Melissa Bell and Jason Herbison have worked in the Australian television industry for several years.

Melissa started work at the age of sixteen, winning a major teen beauty contest. Later, she starred in *Neighbours*, which won Melissa international fame, especially in the United Kingdom. She has appeared in a number of other television series, and is currently working in theatre in the UK.

Jason began writing for television at eighteen. He has written for several television shows including *Neighbours*.

Living Famously

Melissa Bell
&
Jason Herbison

Hodder
Children's
Books

a division of Hodder Headline plc

Copyright © 1995 Melissa Bell and Jason Herbison

First published in Great Britain in 1995
by Hodder Children's Books

This is a fictional diary account of the aims and aspirations of
an ordinary Australian girl who wants to make it big in
television. We have tried to make it as authentic as possible to
convey some insights into how actresses in soap operas live and
work. Accordingly, the background is realistic but our plot and
our characters are all completely imaginary and no reference is
intended to real people, be it those who act in soap operas,
those associated with them or any other person.

A Catalogue record for this book is available from
the British Library

ISBN 0-340-64084-7

Typeset by Avon Dataset Ltd, Bidford-on-Avon

Printed and bound in Great Britain by
Cox & Wyman Ltd, Reading, Berks

Hodder Children's Books
a division of Hodder Headline plc
338 Euston Road
London NW1 3BH

Melanie Entwhistle's star is about to rise . . . but what goes up must come down.

In this, her previously unpublished diary, Melanie lifts the lid on the seedy world of showbusiness.

I dedicate this book to my family, Sherry, Mark, Rebecca, Samantha and Mark O'Dare. Also to my Nan and Pop, Mark and Florence Groves. Without their love, strength and support throughout the years of my life, all this would not be possible.

To my husband, Jason Redlich. May we grow into a tower of strength together and enjoy our journey down that winding road.

Melissa

To the memory of my sister, Janice Herbison Cameron. You may not have a copy, but I know you will read every word.

Jason

October 6

Two thousand calories. Here I am, sitting on the cushion-covered toilet seat, polishing off my fourth piece of chocolate cake and wishing I could flush myself into Sydney Harbour. I'm sure my party will go on without me. I can hear my old East 17 tape on the deck, a positive indication the party is in the dying stages and hormones will be getting the better of everybody. My parents will roll in the driveway any second (an hour early), the garage door will spring open and headlights flash over the pathetic orgy. The Volvo will trip over the badly stashed bottle of gin, prompting the familiar cry, 'What the hell is going on here?' I will be sent to my room, my friends will be sent home and I will be forced to work overtime to cover the damage. My mother will repeat, 'Oh Fred, where did we go wrong?', Sebastian will have a smirk on his face and even the dog will start sneering at me.

The sad thing is, I don't even care. Am I really destined for something better or is my life the sum total of these four floral-papered walls? I try to look on the bright side – I have a few friends (old wounds from high school whose collective life stories wouldn't even cover a toilet roll),

1

a job (waiting tables in a Bondi cafe and taking orders from a slime named Pietro) and a boyfriend, Troy, (who sees his pizza delivery-van as a vehicle to a big, bright future). They're all so happy with their boring, mundane lives. They think the world revolves round the North Shore, the epitome of decent, moral living. A good upbringing, a good education, every child born with a guarantee. Well, this isn't enough for me. I think there's more to life. I want to see my face on a billboard, turn heads in a crowd and meet people who cop speeding tickets and park illegally outside their therapist. I want to act, I want to sing . . . I want to be seen and heard. I want to have it all. One day I will. This is, after all, the beginning of a new phase in my life.

Happy Birthday Melanie Entwhistle.

October 7

8.30a.m.   Sydney Harbour

So this is how it feels to be nineteen years of age. My hair is going crazy in the wind, last night's pleasure at the lips has put an inch around my hips and my chin is giving birth to a classic zit. The ferry conductor still mentally undressed me when I boarded, the trip across the harbour is bumpy as usual and when I arrive in Circular Quay the bus to Bondi will undoubtedly be late. So I'm late for work, again. Pietro will hit the roof. Crisis. I've just realised the designer bracelet Troy brought me is no longer on my wrist. I know I put it on this morning – it must've fallen off when I was running to catch the ferry. I can hardly go back and look for it now. I don't really like the design, but it came from his heart which will be shattered when he learns I have lost it. Especially after all the trouble he went to last night – helping me to bed because I lied and said I had food poisoning, ordering all my friends home and cleaning up the garage so my parents wouldn't hit the roof. He even wiped the vomit out of the washing-machine, which really says it all about my party.

I have lost the bracelet which he gave me as a symbol of his love, yet he will be more upset about it than me. What does this say about our relationship?

October 8

8.30p.m.   Mosman Manor

I finally told Troy about losing the bracelet. He was disappointed, but understanding. The only positive thing that happened today was my belated birthday present to myself. I saw a fortune-teller named Contessa. She told me the most amazing things! She said the next few days would be very important in the shaping of my future. She muttered something about opportunity, adventure and danger. Standard psychic babble.

October 9

Maxwell McKenzie. He stepped off the sidewalk, looked at my breasts and ordered a strong black coffee. The tip he left is worth a week's wages – an audition for the Miss Bondi beach contest! The big break I've been waiting for! Max is the organiser. He's tall, well dressed, a cross between Harrison Ford and Fred Flintstone. I know, I know . . . I shouldn't get too carried away. But, don't forget, last year's winner, Muffy Miller, is now on that game show, what's it called, *Hit The Spot*? And first prize is one thousand dollars cash, a summer wardrobe and an acting agent. Contessa was right – my life is changing!

I'm convinced my family are out to get me. Dad said, 'I know what goes on at those kind of competitions.' Mum said, 'They don't want you to wear a swimsuit, do they?' Sebastian said I'm too fat to win. Troy had a massive attack about our holiday in Surfers Paradise, but the contest is almost two weeks before so we'll still be able to go. I only wish I wanted to. Miss Bondi is the only thing that matters to me now. Stocktake. I still have to pass an audition, but I will . . . won't I? I mean, I don't really look like a blimp? Crisis: I'm taking tomorrow afternoon off work to audition for Maxwell . . . what am I going to wear? Should I go for the Claudia Schiffer sex kitten, or maybe the sweet, virginal . . . you know, like Olivia Newton John in that old movie, what's it called, *Grease*? I can't stuff this up.

October 10

4.25p.m.   Oxford Street

I'm so excited I could scream – but I don't think the passengers on this bus would appreciate it! I've just been to the auditions – silicon city. I fastened my Wonderbra, strutted my stuff and I'm in! I went for the time bomb look – bursting at the seams, ready to explode. Mad Max selected the ten finalists. I've passed the first test, now I have almost three weeks until the contest. I need a swimsuit, casual wear and a 'wild card'. The first two I shouldn't have a problem with, but the wild card . . . Maxwell wants something different, off-beat.

I wish this bus would hurry up. There seems to be someone holding up the traffic ahead. Oh no. You won't believe this. That someone isn't just anyone. It's Troy in his pizza delivery-van. Five foot seven, college cut and perfect teeth. I'm watching him struggle with an armful of pizzas, while motorists toot their horns and people like me sit here and abuse him. I know he's doing it all for me. Working extra hours to pay for the bracelet I lost, build some kind of future . . . and here I am, building a different future in which he doesn't figure.

October 11

Bondi Beach is a hive of activity. I'm supposed to be working but I can't keep my eyes off the spot where the stage will be set for the contest. I still can't believe I am in the running. Nadine gave me a hard time about it. She reckons the contest is demeaning to women. Well, I know it is but I'm only doing it as a passport to bigger and better things. The real appeal is the prize of an acting agent, which is worth any amount of public humiliation. There's nothing wrong with that, is there? I have to go. The customers are getting restless.

October 12

8.30p.m. *Mosman Manor*

I'm really spinning out about this wild card number. After finding nothing on Oxford Street, I checked out Mum's wardrobe hoping to find some time-warped seventies flashback which I could pass off as the latest Parisian design. Problem is, she's such a blimp I'd have to sew it all into proportion. Even the buttons have stretch marks. I've just done the Cindy Crawford workout. Agony!

October 13

Today has been the worst day in my life. OK, maybe I'm being a little over dramatic. Pietro gave me a huge lecture about lifting my game. He reckons I'm preoccupied with the contest and neglecting my work. He's right! I couldn't care less about Pietro, the cafe or the people who come into it. I managed to calm him down, but one thing I know for sure – I have to win the contest and quit that hellhole.

I had lunch with Troy – pizza of course – the first time I've seen him in a couple of days. He talked non-stop about our trip to Surfers Paradise. Nadine, Karen and Shane are also pumped up about it. The more I think about it, the more I don't want to go. Thing is, they are my friends and I was looking forward to it when we first came up with the idea. But I'm not the person I was back then.

October 14

11.41p.m.

I just got a call from Maxwell McKenzie. He's invited me out to dinner this coming Thursday night! I wouldn't be surprised if there are strings attached, but I can't see the harm in going, if only for a laugh. I wouldn't do anything, of course. Crisis. Troy is also expecting me at his parents' house for dinner. It's their twenty-fifth anniversary. What am I going to do?

October 15

This diary belongs to the ultimate bitch. I told Troy I couldn't go to his parents' tomorrow night because I have chronic period pains. Nothing makes him more sympathetic than this. I never used to lie to Troy, but now I'm doing it all the time. If I can't tell him the truth . . . does this mean our relationship is a lie? This dinner with Maxwell is just too important. I must make a good impression, not just to win the contest but to show I am serious about making it to the top. Who knows what else he could do to help my career? Sure, I feel bad about Troy. But I can't spend the whole night feeling guilty. I'm going to have the time of my life. Crisis: I hope I can keep Max under control. Solution: I'll pack the mace, keep a padlock on my panties and scream if I am in danger.

October 16

11.55p.m.   *Mosman Manor*

I have had the best night. There were lots of other people at dinner. A record producer, Dale Starling, though I can't believe that's his real name. A stuntman, I think his name was Harley. There was also this girl, Annabella, a model. Her lips are on that billboard just over the harbour bridge on the Opera House side. She's also entering the contest. To be completely honest, she may have nice lips but the rest of her is pretty standard. She's got these bug eyes which kind of rotate after the first glass of champagne. Even so, she's really sweet. Max kept topping up my glass. I had this feeling he was trying to get me legless so he could jump me. Then he dropped the bombshell – he's married! He and his wife have this, um, 'open' relationship. I was positive he was going to make a move on me but, at the end of the night, he simply gave me a kiss on the cheek and wished me luck on the big day. I'd love to tell you more about it but I'm feeling a bit sick . . .

October 17

10.00a.m.   *Bondi Beach*

I am sitting on the sand. My head is throbbing and my stomach feels like it is about to explode. Worse than this, I have just been fired. That's right. I roll up for work, Pietro takes one look at my bloodshot eyes and tells me to hit the pavement. Guess I had a little too much to drink last night. Mum and Dad are going to kill me. My bank account has never looked worse and I'm so immobile I'm likely to get washed away with the tide. My world is suddenly upside down . . .

8.30p.m.   *Mosman Manor*

Mum and Dad hit the roof. They told me to go back to Pietro and withdraw my resignation which, unbeknown to them, is a little hard since he actually fired me. Troy

9

was more supportive, in a typically impassive way: 'Whatever you want to do,' he mumbled.

October 18

7.30p.m.   Mosman Manor

The first day of my unemployment. I awoke at nine-thirty, went for a power walk round the block then spent an hour in the sun. I had a light salad for lunch (much healthier than the tempting food at the cafe) then trotted off to the gym for a cardio funk class. The only mistake I made was spending the afternoon with Mum. I gave her a hard time about discouraging my dreams, so she felt guilty and insisted on helping me with my wild card number. Predictably, we both had completely opposing ideas about style and price – I want something over the top, revealing yet tantalising. Mum would rather have me wear a tent.

Troy is due here any minute. I feel really guilty about lying to him the other night. I feel even worse about the trip to Surfers Paradise. Troy has his heart set on it. The more I think about it, the more I know I can't go. If I lose the contest I will be miserable. If I win I'll want to stay here. Troy is bringing a pizza (a special low calorie version) over tonight. I'll tell him I can't go. Simple as that.

10.50p.m.   Mosman Manor

The pizza was on the table. I was about to break the news. Then I open the box. There, among the anchovies, was

10

another bracelet – a replacement for the one I lost. Troy has been working late deliveries all week to pay for it. How could I possibly tell him I don't want to go to Surfers – after all he's done for me?

October 19

2.30a.m.   Mosman Manor

I've just had the most bizarre dream. No, it was a nightmare. Troy and I were married, living in a house, a bit like the one round the corner. I could hear children screaming, the kettle boiling, dog barking in the backyard. The interior was a shambles – stuffed toys were littered everywhere, dirty washing was draped on the floor and a gigantic rat nibbled at a pizza on the kitchen table. Troy looked a hundred years old. Then I caught a glimpse of myself in the mirror – tatty clothes, child-bearing hips, with another on the way. Is this my future?

October 20

11.55p.m.   Nadine's house

Yesterday began with a nightmare and today is ending with one. I agreed to a night of social suicide – clubbing with the girls. Voni, Nadine, Kim and Karen dragged me off to PMT. I have never felt so humiliated in my life. The bouncer refused to let us in. I could tell he wanted to let me through, but not the girls – *so* North Shore: all one pint screamers with sensible shoes. That look is completely against the law on the east side. Voni decided she wanted to argue. Kim tried her usual 'Do you know my father's a high court judge?' while Nadine and I counted blood stains on the pavement. Ours would surely be next. There was also this really strange guy lurking behind the door, I can't describe him. He was not that attractive, but he had this aura, this presence – all directed at me. At least I think so. Anyway, I'm at Nadine's place now. We left Voni, Kim and Karen dancing at Flashlight. That place is tragic. I wish someone would blow up the North Shore. Almost makes me want to move to Tasmania.

October 21

8.30p.m.   Mosman Manor

I have had a fantastic day. Annabella – the other contestant I met at dinner on Thursday night – came over. She is so switched on! She entered the contest last year (but had to pull out at the last minute) which made her a prime candidate for an interrogation from Mum. Mum and Dad are both convinced the contest will corrupt me, that the organisers are on drugs and I will be enticed into their world of debauchery. Annabella assured her the contest is all above board: 'A great opportunity to build confidence, presentation skills and win fantastic prizes to share with the entire family.' The real incentive came when Mum realised Annabella's mother is a rival at tennis –

Mum would do anything to beat her. If I win the contest, as opposed to Annabella, Mum could crow about the victory for weeks. She's now my biggest supporter. Annabella also offered to help me with my wild card number. I'm not sure why she wants to help – considering we are both rivals – except for the possibility that she really is a nice, genuine person.

October 22

7.45p.m.   Mosman Manor

I'm looking and feeling terrific. Annabella and I spent the whole day on Oxford Street, sitting in cafes and acting like we own the copyright on having a good time. Her mobile phone rang constantly! She seemed to know just about every cute guy who walked past. We also looked at a few wild cards and I think I've found the dress I simply have to wear. I asked the shop assistant to put it on hold as I'm not sure if I can afford it. My bank account is looking pretty dire and without a job it can only get worse. But the dress is stunning. Annabella says it's an investment for the future. The thousand dollars prize money will pay it off. I'll think about that tomorrow – I've got more exciting plans for tonight. Annabella's invited me to some cocktail party, which I'm sure will explode. Oh yeah, Troy. I won't tell him if you don't.

October 23 & 24

I have so much to tell you! The last couple of days have been a mad mix of parties, places and famous faces. I have spent the whole time with Annabella. The cocktail party was great. I met all these models, names I didn't know but faces I have seen everywhere. I felt like such a nothing compared to them all. More incentive for me to win the contest. On that score, Annabella has been incredibly helpful. We went back to the shop where I have the dress on hold and she haggled the price right down. I bought it! More than I can afford, but I'll look great. Better than Annabella, which is what I can't work out. She seems to be helping me to beat her. I suppose the contest doesn't mean that much to her. She already has an agent and lots of work – her portfolio is amazing. I also told her I want to be an actress rather than a model so I guess this makes me less threatening. Reality check. I haven't spoken to Troy over the last couple of days. Amidst all this fun and excitement I forgot I have a boyfriend!

October 25

5.30p.m.   *Mosman Manor*

I'm just back from contest rehearsal. Nerve-wracking! Maxwell talked us through the three sections, one for each wardrobe change. There is also a pause where we talk about ourselves – our interests and concerns. Three things I won't be talking about – the environment, children and world hunger! I'm going to get up there and be completely honest. I care about . . . myself.

October 26

8.45p.m.   Mosman Manor

I just popped over to Troy's place. I felt bad about neglecting him so I thought I'd see how he was going. His face lit up when I walked in the door. He is so in love with me. He is even doing extra deliveries so he can afford to take me to top restaurants in Surfers. My feelings for Troy are like a rollercoaster. One minute I feel suffocated, the next I think he's the sweetest guy in the universe. Maybe I should write a list of the positives and negatives:

Positives	Negatives
Honest	Poor fashion sense
Generous	Cowlicks in hair
Compassionate	Smells of pizza
Hard-working	
Loyal	
Loving	

I think the positives slightly outweigh the negatives. If I know this, why am I having doubts? Do I simply want someone better to come along? If so, what kind of person does this make me? Don't just sit there, say something!

October 27

6.45p.m.   Mosman Manor

It's really hit the fan. The worst possible thing has happened: Mum and Dad found some coke – yes, as in cocaine, the illegal substance – in the pocket of my denim jacket. I can't believe it! I don't know how it got there. Could somebody have put it there by mistake? The last time I wore it was, um . . . to the cocktail party with Annabella. I had it on the entire night. Surely I would have known if someone had slipped it in. And why would they give it away in the first place? Hold on . . . I also wore it to dinner the other night with Maxwell. I slipped it off . . . Yeah, now I remember. Max dropped it in the cloakroom for me. Wait a minute . . . Max couldn't have put it there, could he? I did sort of play along when they were all talking about 'doing lines', even though I've never done one in my life. I don't even know what doing a line means, only that it has something to do with drugs. Maybe he thought he was giving me a treat?

Mum and Dad are talking it over, deciding whether they believe I am innocent or whether they will dish out a severe punishment. I'll have to give them some kind of explanation.

8.30p.m.   Mosman Manor

I'm in tears. Mum and Dad have ordered me to pull out of the contest. They think the cocaine is evidence – regardless of the fact I didn't use it – that my new ambitions are running me off the rails. They feel my welfare is at risk. I know they mean well, but I am nineteen and can take care of myself. I've made up my mind. I'm not dropping out.

October 28

6.15p.m.   Annabella's flat

I can't believe this is happening to me. I told Mum and Dad I was persevering with the contest, so they kicked me out of the house! They thought it would pressure me into backing down. Instead, I rang Annabella. She's a lifesaver. She came over and helped me pack a bag. That's right – I've left home. Well, not permanently. I will stay here until the contest is over. Hopefully things will have calmed down and I can return. I can't believe the contest is tomorrow. Tomorrow! How can I possibly get up on stage tomorrow?

10.55p.m.

My head is spinning. One minute I am getting ready to go to bed, the next Annabella kicks me out of her apartment. I'm slowly putting it all together – the reason why Annabella was so nice to me, encouraging me to turn my back on my parents and Troy. She was setting me up to be dependent on her, so she could turn her back on me – the night before the contest! The one night when I need a good, long sleep, a comfortable bed and a place to shower in the morning. I feel like such a fool. I also found out Annabella was responsible for planting the coke in my jacket. All designed to cause conflict with my parents. She has succeeded. I don't want to go home, I don't want to see Troy. I have no one to turn to. I'm too ashamed to call my friends, I have no other family worth mentioning. Miss Bondi has lost her crown – before she has even won it.

Midnight   Kings Cross

I have found a bed for the night. I am staying in a hostel. It's cheap, it's dirty, but at least I have my own room and a bed to sleep on. Now I am going to cry myself to sleep.

October 29

12.15p.m.   Bondi Beach

One hour to go. I am sitting in the backstage tent, with my old dressing-gown over my bikini, having very serious second thoughts. I haven't been or called home all morning. There are no helicopters in the sky, so I assume my parents have convinced themselves I'm OK. Troy probably doesn't know any of this yet. Annabella is outside soaking up a few final moments of sun. She hasn't even asked where I ended up last night. I could have been raped, hit by a bus or washed up on the beach and she wouldn't have batted an eyelid. The other girls are busy getting ready. They're all surrounded by parents and friends, increasing my feeling of loneliness. Crisis. My dress! My dress has just popped out of Ursula Winter's bag! She must be planning to wear it as her wild card. Just when I thought today couldn't get any worse. This is an omen. The final straw.

2.25p.m.

I can't believe I'm doing this. I've survived the first heat. I think I impressed the judges with my casual wear, despite Annabella's attempt to trip me on the runway. The crowd thought it was part of the routine so I managed to come out looking pretty good. My real downfall is yet to come. The wild card section. I spoke to Ursula and – surprise, surprise – Annabella encouraged her to buy that same dress! She set us both up. Ursula is on stage before me, so she'll get to make the first entrance in the dress – which means it'll look like I have copied her. What am I going to do? I can hear Maxwell winding up. We'll be back out there any minute. This is crazy – I can't go out there. What am I going to do?

5.30p.m.

I have a million things to tell you, but I am so excited I can hardly keep my pen still to write. I don't know where to begin. I thought my chances were over, so I ripped up the dress. Then Troy showed up – yes, at the very last minute – and convinced me I had to go out there. He helped me put the dress back together with a few safety pins. Out I went. Everybody loved me! Max described my dress as 'hot off the Paris catwalks'! I also saw Mum and Dad standing in the crowd, cheering me on. Suddenly, I was glowing, confident – a winner! All the other girls talked about ocean pollution and unemployment but I was completely honest about my interests and concerns. I talked about communication problems between parents and children, about striving for your dreams. I nearly died when Annabella and I made the top two. I thought she was going to win, but then Maxwell read out my name. Muffy Miller put the crown on my head. I felt like a princess. I have won! Mum and Dad came up afterwards, saying they were really proud of me. No hard feelings. Mum's also happy because she has a victory over Annabella's old lady. I haven't got time to write any more. I'm on my way to the Miss Bondi party. I'll tell you all about it.

October 30

4.30p.m.   Mosman Manor

I have just woken up. The sun is streaming through the blinds. I can hear the sound of my father mowing the lawn and the ferry docking at the pier. I have had the most amazing dream. I dreamt I won the Miss Bondi title, that I went to this fantastic party . . . wait a minute, that was no dream. The crown is lying on the floor of my room, my face is stained with congratulatory kisses . . . I really did win!

The party I thought I'd dreamt really was at the Swiss Grand in Double Bay, one of Sydney's finest. I stepped out of the limousine and had my photo taken, before being escorted to the reception room. All eyes were upon me. The place was decked out with lavish food, champagne, celebrities swanning about. Stars from all the shows, models, wannabes. I used to fall in the last category, but last night I actually felt like someone. Max smiled like a proud father, though it was my real father who stole my heart. I could see genuine pride in his eyes. Mum, Sebastian and Troy were equally supportive, though a bit overwhelmed by the fanfare. They said nothing about Annabella, no 'We told you so' or 'Don't ever do that again'. They were simply happy for me. Max introduced me to Sue-Ellen, the head booker from Quinn Dexter's agency. She talked at a million miles, full of big plans, things I have to do, people I have to see. Andre Blewitt, the actor from *Barossa Towers*, presented me with my prizes and I had to make a speech. I had made it, I didn't have to worry any more. I don't know what happened to the rest of the night, just that I had the time of my life.

October 31

10.00p.m.   Mosman Manor

I've spent the entire day run off my feet, racing all over the city. The day began with an appointment at Quinn

Dexter's. The waiting-room was full of famous faces. The receptionist gave me a coffee with low fat milk and no sugar. She told me that Sue-Ellen would be with me shortly. I sat there, overwhelmed, imagining my face on the wall. Sue-Ellen finally appeared and invited me into her office. She sat behind an enormous glass-top desk, with just a telephone and a note pad on it. She bombarded me with my tasks for the next few weeks. I have to have my head shots done so I can go see all the casting agents. 'Go see' means to drop in, show them who I am and do a general spiel as opposed to a set audition. Sue-Ellen also suggested I enrol in some acting classes. More importantly, she wants me to get a mobile phone. I must be contactable! She mentioned a few upcoming jobs that I may be suitable to test for. Nothing much can happen until Sue-Ellen can organise a photographer, so I'll spend the next couple of days fulfilling my Miss Bondi commitments. I'll tell you about them tomorrow.

November 1

3.30p.m.   Pietro's Cafe

The life of Miss Bondi is not an easy one. Publicity appearances, interviews . . . OK, one appearance and one interview! The appearance was at the Bondi Beach Surf Club, where I had to have lunch with the sponsors of the club and have my photograph taken with the lifeguards. The guys formed a human pyramid, with me perched on top. They were all adorable – golden brown suntans, bulging biceps and innocent smiles. I had a wild time.

The interview was for the *Eastern Suburbs Gazette*. Of course, it was no accident that I chose this cafe to do it in. I wanted Pietro to see how far I had come. He stood behind the coffee machine, trying not to look at me. I know he was burning with jealousy.

The reporter asked questions about how it felt to be Miss Bondi, as well as my relationship status and future plans. I'd fantasised so many times about what to say in an interview like this, but when I was actually doing it, I felt totally unprepared. I think I said some really stupid things!

November 2

8.30p.m.   Mosman Manor

'Melanie Entwhistle – The Most Beautiful Miss Bondi in History!' That's the headline on the front page of the *Gazette*, complete with my smiling photo. I made the front page! Dad was so proud he went and bought a stack load of copies. Sebastian has been stealing them out of everyone's letter boxes! I was recognised three times by the general public, admittedly outside newsagencies where I was busy stocking up on copies. I don't know how people can complain about the price of fame – I feel great!

November 3

I have spent the entire day with Troy. He is very excited about our holiday to Surfers – I wish I were as well. I still haven't told Sue-Ellen I am going. The trip is only for a week and a half, but that's a long time in the world of showbusiness – who knows what I will miss out on. I can't back out – it would break Troy's heart.

I still have a few days in Sydney, so I intend to kickstart my career as much as possible in that time. Sue-Ellen has organised the agency photo shoot for tomorrow. The photographer's name is Jerry DeMont. I have to be at his studio in Surrey Hills at eight in the morning. I can't wait!

November 4

1.30p.m.   Jerry's Studio

I can't wait for this ordeal to be over! I thought having my photo taken in a studio would be exciting, but the process is long, uncomfortable and tiring. Jerry has allowed me the luxury of a short lunch break. I am writing to keep my mind off food – the clothes are so tight that I'm not going to eat for the next month.

Jerry is interesting. Physically, he's a cross between Brad Pitt and Big Bird. Sue, the make-up artist, is a total bitch. She treats me like I'm a piece of mutton she must dress up as lamb. I have to admit the novelty is fast wearing off.

I have to stand in front of a blinding light, twisting and turning my face in ways I never thought possible. Jerry is very patient, easing my nervousness with jokes and healthy pointers. He's calling me back now. Later.

November 5

5.00p.m.   *Mosman Manor*

I'm not sure if this is good or bad news: I can go to Surfers. Sue-Ellen can't get me any casting appointments until the week after next, so I can't do much until then – except hop on a bus and have a wacky, zany time with my friends. I really have no excuse for backing out.

I have bought a whizz-bang mobile phone, which I'm charging right now. Sue-Ellen will have no cause to phone me at home, so she'll never know where I am. As far as the agency is concerned, I may as well be in Sydney.

November 6

7.30p.m.   *Mosman Manor*

Two more sleeps until Surfers Paradise! I'm actually feeling a little excited about it. I've allowed myself to get caught up in the Miss Bondi hype over the last few weeks so much so I've forgotten about my friends and the fun times we planned together. I'm sure I'll be able to recapture that spirit. None of us are going out tonight or tomorrow. We're conserving all our energy.

November 7

I should be in bed. Troy's parents are driving us to the bus stop at five in the morning. Nadine, Karen and Shane will be there to meet us. Mum and Dad just gave me a huge lecture about behaving myself, i.e. not doing anything 'untoward' with Troy. Karen, Nadine and I are sharing a room. To be honest, I'm quite happy to do that. Troy has other ideas. Sex. We have come close to doing it a few times, but I never felt right. Is there something wrong with me?

November 8

Midday   Pacific Highway

Six hours into the trip. Troy is talking to Nadine so I have five minutes to think. Despite my determination to enjoy myself, I'm having a miserable time. All I can think about is Jerry's photos. I can't wait to see them and to get out there and strut my stuff. I have often wondered what it would be like if my career did take off and I was known all round the world in everyone's homes. How will it change me? For the moment, I'm reading Strasberg's *At the Actor's Studio*. Although I can't be in Sydney, I'm following Sue-Ellen's instructions and polishing my act. I suddenly feel inspired to write some poetry.

If I could see the future
I would be on top of the world
But I don't know what's next
Though I will do my very best
It's the beginning of the new me
I hope I pass the test!

November 9

7.00p.m.   *Surfers Paradise*

At long last, the big, bright, tacky lights of Surfers Paradise.
High-rise apartments, flashing neon signs in Japanese. And
I'm here with my friends: Nadine, my devoted confidante;
Karen and Shane, the epitome of a happy couple; and
Troy, my dearly beloved boyfriend. After fourteen hours
on the bus I feel like killing all of them!

10.45p.m.   *The Purple Panther*

The Purple Panther. I can't believe we're staying in a motel
with a flashing, fluorescent purple panther watching over
the No Vacancy sign. We were greeted by a local with a
broad Australian accent, giving a stiff warning about
drinking and impossible instructions to find our rooms.
Troy and Shane are in the suite next door. Karen, Nadine
and I are squashed into one half the size. All I want to do
is find the pool and drown myself. I think Troy is looking
for some love and affection, but I've got only one thing
to say to him: Somebody get me out of here!

November 10

8.30p.m.   *The Purple Panther*

Ocean World, Water World, Fantasy World – my world is over! I have spent all day sight-seeing, catching shuttle buses to the tackiest fun parks on earth and going on rides which make my stomach drop at every twist and fall. Everyone else is having a great time, but I am miserable. I know I sound like a killjoy, but I am making an effort – Troy thinks I'm having the time of my life. I'm a very good actress. But I don't think I can keep the act up much longer. Later.

November 11

10.00p.m.   *The Purple Panther*

Another day in paradise. I am suffering from food poisoning, the legacy of a master pig-out in an all-you-can-eat Chinese restaurant. The others are at some night club called Shark Alarm. I thought I'd give it a miss. Hang on, Melanie. This isn't the attitude. I suppose I could enjoy myself if I really tried. Pledge time: I'm going to have a good time tomorrow, no matter what. I'm going to enjoy every minute of my time in Surfers Paradise.

November 12

Newsflash: Sue-Ellen called on the mobile (the first time it has rung). I have an audition for *Mercy Hospital*! Yes, as in the top-rated super soap! Jerry – the guy who did my agency shots – also shoots for the show and he thought I had such a good look he told the producer! The producer agreed and they have called me in. Sue-Ellen says this is practically unheard of. I'm not even a member of Actors Equity (the union) and she was only planning to send me for commercials. Now I'm up for a role in my favourite TV show! I am now on a plane to Sydney.

I didn't even say goodbye to Troy. I gave Nadine a note to pass on which read, 'Dear Troy, The big break I have been dreaming about has finally come. I have to rush back to Sydney. I will phone you. All my love, Melanie.' Thinking back over the note, it sounds so cold and heartless but I truly didn't know what to say. I can't think about it now – I have a chance to turn my dream into reality.

8.30p.m.   *Mosman Manor*

I'm home. I have my audition script for *Mercy Hospital*. I'm going for the part of Sasha Somers, the long-lost daughter of Edwina Somers. She's a nurse. The character breakdown describes her as 'a bright, happy-go-lucky eighteen year old'. The script is full of complicated medical terms, but I have the family medical book out and am determined to get it right. The audition is at one tomorrow. I can't believe this!

November 13

3.45p.m.   Mosman Jetty

I've blown it. I've stuffed up my big chance of winning a part in *Mercy Hospital*. I jumbled my lines, knocked the camera off the stand and made the mistake of wearing red. Sue-Ellen forgot to tell me it bleeds when you wear it on screen. The camera has trouble defining red and it looks like you've been pelted with rotten tomatoes. She also forgot to tell me the audition was in a tiny little room, with just myself and the casting director to play the other part. The casting director didn't really say anything when I left, but I got the message loud and clear: 'Don't call us, we'll call you.' I could tell they thought I was all wrong for the part – too fat, too short, too immature. They hated me. I hate me. On top of this, I get home to find a message from Troy. Mum said he sounded very upset on the phone. He has every right to be. His girlfriend disappears during a holiday they have been looking forward to all year without so much as saying goodbye or explaining her reasons in person. Now the audition has been such a disaster I wish I'd never flown back. I have made a fool of myself, hurt the person I love – all for nothing. I deserve to fall off this jetty and sink to the bottom of the harbour.

November 14

7.55p.m.   Mosman Manor

I slept for fourteen hours last night. Every time my eyes
threatened to awaken, I turned myself over and escaped
into the safety of my pillow. When Sebastian decided to
play his Pearl Jam CD at full volume, I could no longer
deny the world outside; I had to get up and face it. I sat
in front of the television. This only made me feel worse.
Tonight's episode of *Mercy Hospital* was plugged during
every commercial break, a painful reminder of what I have
missed out on. Troy phoned again this afternoon, but I
refused to take the call. I don't know what to say to him.

November 15

10.00p.m.   Mosman Manor

Nadine just phoned from Surfers Paradise. She says Troy
is really upset and confused about my disappearance,
drinking more than he can handle and blaming himself
for whatever he thinks has gone wrong. But he is not to
blame. This is all my fault. I feel terrible.

November 16

12.15p.m.   Mosman Manor

I have spoken to Troy. I told him I was sorry, that I have
been selfish and want to make it up to him. He didn't say

much, in fact, he didn't say anything. I could tell he was dreadfully hungover. I told him I would try to fly back to Surfers and rejoin them for the last couple of days of the holiday. I have almost nothing left from the thousand dollars prize money so I'll have to hit Mum and Dad for a loan to pay for the flight.

I wish I could say this act is entirely selfless, that I am doing it for Troy and not for myself. Truth is, I have to leave Sydney. I know I wasn't having a good time up in Surfers, but that was because I was clinging to the hopeless fantasy of a glamorous career back here. Now I realise this will never happen.

November 17

2.30p.m.   Charles Kingford Smith Airport

I'm on stand-by for the next flight to Surfers Paradise. I missed a seat on the last plane, but there is another in about half an hour. Mum and Dad have no idea I have left. The mobile has been ringing all day. I'm sure it's Troy but I don't want to answer. I just want to get back to Surfers, fall into his arms and make everything all right. There it goes again. I'll have to answer.

3.00p.m.   Inner city

I'm in a cab on the way home. It wasn't Troy on the phone, it was Sue-Ellen. The most incredible thing has happened – I have call back for *Mercy Hospital*! Apparently they were really impressed and I have made the short list. I cannot believe it. Everything was going wrong – now everything is going right. I have a second chance. I'm not going to stuff this up (why do I get the feeling I have written this before?). Don't worry I haven't forgotten about Troy. I'll think about him tomorrow. After the audition.

November 18

2.30p.m.   Mosman Manor

The audition went really well. They asked me to wear a nurse's uniform to see if I look the part. Then I had to do a cold read; I had fifteen minutes to learn the scene, which was full of even more unpronounceable medical terms. Somehow I got my tongue round them. This time, there was another guy as well as the casting director. I'm not sure who he was, but he looked important. As for Troy, I phoned The Purple Panther to tell him the good news. He wasn't there. I left a message.

November 19

8.45p.m.   Mosman Manor

The waiting game. I haven't heard a word from *Mercy Hospital*. I have no idea if they liked me or not. I know Sue-Ellen does. She sent me for a dog food commercial this afternoon. I had to hold the tin right up to my nose – I feel sick just thinking about it. In a funny kind of way, I hope I don't get it. I have this fantasy mapped out in my head that I'll get on a soap, cut a record, make a movie then retire to a villa in the South of France. A tacky dog commercial tends to shatter the strategy! I'm desperate to hear something about *Mercy Hospital*. I hope I do tomorrow.

November 20

10.00a.m.   *Mosman Manor*

Here I go again. *Mercy Hospital* want me for yet another audition! Sue-Ellen said I'm down to the final three. Now they want me to read against the guy who may play my love interest, just to see how we look and if we get along. They are even sending a cab to pick me up and take me there. I think I can hear someone pulling up now. I'm looking out of the window. Sure enough, it's my cab. Wait . . . I don't like who is getting out. It's Troy! I forgot he was getting back today.

10.45a.m.   *Inner city*

I'm in the cab on my way to the audition. My mascara has run down my face, my eyes are puffy, I look a total mess. Troy is so upset with me. I'm upset with him for upsetting me. I know I owe him an apology but he picked the wrong morning to come looking for it. We argued, I said things I didn't mean and he said things I didn't want to hear. Now I'm off to the biggest audition of my life.

1.30p.m.   *Mosman Manor*

I'm back from the audition. I read against this guy named Norton Weilburg. I don't know, *some* people might find his wicked grin attractive, but, for me, red hair and a serious lack of muscle – not to mention height – is a real turn-off. If you ask me, he brought my performance right down. All I want to do is go home and go to bed . . . forget about the audition, forget about Troy.

November 21

10.45a.m.   *Mosman Manor*

I am in a state of shock. Just when I thought my life was over, I find it is just beginning. I have won the part of Sasha Somers on *Mercy Hospital*! I have made it! I just got the call from Sue-Ellen. I have to rush into the agency. The contract is waiting for me! This is it! I have made the BIG time!

6.45p.m.   *Mosman Manor*

Today has been the most incredible day of my life. I know I said that about my sixteenth birthday, the New Kids On The Block concert and winning the Miss Bondi title but this time I really mean it. Sue-Ellen guided me through the contract, including a couple of changes she wants to make. I am signed for six months with a six month option, in their favour. This means, after six months, the show has the option to keep me or let me go. The money is amazing – four times what I used to earn at Pietro's Cafe in a week. I also get transport to and from Channel Five, which is on the other side of town. I start shooting 'location' in a couple of weeks. Location refers to all the outside shots, while interiors are filmed in the studio. Location is shot the week before studio, even though all the scenes appear in one episode. Confusing, I know.

I phoned Troy – the first time we have talked since yesterday – and invited him over to a celebration dinner. Nadine, Karen and Shane are also coming. I have a feeling everything is going to be all right.

10.45p.m.   Mosman Manor

I can hardly keep my eyes open. Everyone has just left. Mum cooked a great dinner, Dad cracked open his best bottle of champagne and even Sebastian was happy for me. I couldn't quite work out what was going through Troy's head. He didn't say much, but he wasn't angry. Like me, I think he is a bit overwhelmed.

November 22

7.45p.m.   Mosman Manor

I am on the biggest high of my life. I spent today at Channel Five meeting everyone who is anyone. Casper Donald, the producer, welcomed me with a warm hug. He's got a touch of the Maxwell McKenzie's about him, but seems harmless. I also met the publicist, Tamara Bennett. She's new to the job, but I'd say she's got her eye on the top – and she wants to get there *fast*. I have to go back and see her in a couple of days. Then I had a tour round the studio. The sets are nothing like I expected. They are all so small and dilapidated. They were shooting an operation scene using tomato sauce and sausages as substitutes for blood and body organs. Norma Applegate threw a mad tantrum in the middle of it, complaining that the extra playing the patient was wriggling. Casper introduced me to Norma when the scene was over. I'd say she was in her forties. She's got long dark hair which she wears up in a bun – kind of severe-looking. She plays my mother, so we'll be working together a great deal. Norma was a bit abrupt, then again, she was in a bad mood. I hope we get along. I also got my scripts for the first three weeks – heavy stuff!

Apparently, they have cast some guy named David Davidson in the part of the new doctor, my love interest. Thank God it's not Norton Weilburg, the guy I auditioned with. I hope David is good-looking! I wonder how Troy will feel about me doing love scenes with another guy!

November 23

10.00p.m.   *Mosman Manor*

Troy has just walked out the door – forever. Just when I thought we were getting back on track, he tells me it's over. He said we were 'going in different directions; our future is no longer the same.' He said all the things I was thinking, the words I have written a hundred times in this diary. The words I thought I would be saying to him, not the other way round. The worst thing is, I don't feel that way any more. Through the course of the last few weeks – winning the contest, the trip to Surfers – I actually feel I need him. But he doesn't need me. I guess it's true what they say. You really don't know what you had until you lose it.

November 24

8.00p.m.   Mosman Manor

I am exhausted. I have spent the entire day with Flora Meadows, the acting coach from *Mercy Hospital*. I have to see her every second day until I start taping. She's a cantankerous old drama queen. I had to run through the scenes for my first episode. She said I was terrible. She said my delivery was flat, my projection weak and my facial gyrations over the top. She also sent me home with some voice tapes which I am supposed to be listening to now. There is only one good thing to come out of today. I am so upset with Flora I haven't had time to think about Troy.

November 25

7.15p.m.   Mosman Manor

I have just been over to Troy's place. I thought I'd better give the bracelet back, though secretly I was hoping he would have a change of heart and want to kiss and make up. There was no suggestion of this. Instead, an icy distance. As though we were strangers. I am lying in bed, trying to learn my lines. This should be the happiest time of my life yet I am fighting back the tears. Looking back over this diary, my words make me think I should be happy about breaking up with Troy. I guess I was writing from my head, rather than my heart. I can't go on like this.

November 26

8.35p.m.   Mosman Manor

I have had a fantastic day. I awoke bright and early and went out for a run. I'm going to be trim, taut and terrific by the time I slip into that nurse's uniform. Then I met Flora for a session. I gave it all I had, focused all my energy into the lines and became Sasha Somers. Flora said I'd made a slight improvement, which is a lot coming from her. The production secretary gave me several tapes of the show so I can watch and get a feel for it. I've been watching them all evening. I pinch myself every time I realise I will be up there very soon.

November 27

10.00p.m.   Mosman Manor

I'm lucky to be alive! Tamara trapped me in her office and fired a barrage of questions all afternoon; what I do in my spare time, all about my family and friends. She asked if I had a boyfriend. This was the first time I'd thought about Troy all day, but I covered myself well and said I was single. She has organised a photo shoot for *Exclusive* magazine tomorrow. I'll get to meet my co-star, David Davidson. It feels funny meeting him for the first time at a photo shoot, but I suppose that's the way it goes. Jerry will be taking the shots. A journalist will also be there to interview us. I hope I don't have to talk about Miss Bondi. The beauty queen tag feels a little bit embarrassing now I have moved on to bigger and better things. I wanted to win Miss Bondi so badly at the time – now it pales into insignificance. I suppose, when I make it to Hollywood, I will feel the same way about *Mercy Hospital*. Listen to me! I haven't even started filming and I'm already planning my first feature film!

November 28

7.45p.m.   Mosman Manor

What's in a name? Everything when you're cursed with a title like Norton Weilburg, which is why he changed it to David Davidson! The idiot from the audition somehow managed to get the part of Vince. I didn't have time to recover from the shock of this before Jerry and the *Exclusive* journalist blasted on to the scene, and Tamara insisted we look like a happy couple.

I was pleased to see Jerry and made sure I thanked

him. After all, if Jerry hadn't shown Casper the shots he took of me for the agency, I wouldn't have the job at all. We did the shoot in the operating-theatre set, with David writhing on the table and me, dressed as Sasha the nurse, performing a frontal lobotomy. Quite funny when you think about it . . . The journalist didn't show much interest in us. She held out her tape-recorder and said, 'OK honey, what's your story?' I launched into my well rehearsed pitch, while she yawned as though she had heard it all before. Tamara was happy with my answers, but David didn't impress her. He forgot the name of his character and got confused about his purpose in the show, much to the journalist's amusement. I hope I am able to work with him . . .

November 29

7.45p.m.   Mosman Manor

Panic stations. Juanita Philips, who plays Suzanne on *Mercy*, has a bad back – again – and has to take time off. So all the scenes have been rescheduled. I start location *tomorrow* – one week early! I have to be at the Botany Bay Hospital – the real life exterior for Mercy Hospital – at six a.m. The studio rushed out a schedule. My scenes are all out of order. In the storyline, Sasha gets hit by a wayward bus as she is arriving at the hospital. There is a big stunt involved and the show can only afford one take. I have only one chance to get it right! I rushed in to see Flora and we rehearsed the scenes. I shouldn't have any problem remembering the lines, but I feel so nervous. What if I stuff up? What if I fluff my words during the crash scene? What if the scene is unusable and they have to crash another bus, costing thousands of dollars?

November 30

9.30p.m.   Mosman Manor

I have never worked so hard in my life. Today has been one pressure cooker after another. I honestly don't know if I should laugh or cry. I arrived on time, only to find half my scenes had been rewritten. Apparently, they couldn't afford to crash a bus so it turned into a mounted police horse. Sasha gets run over by a horse! They had a stunt double, but only for the actual accident. David was impossible to work with. He was supposed to witness the accident, come rushing out of the hospital and say: 'Young lady, are you all right?' Not a hard line, but do you think David could get his tongue round it? Not a chance. I'm kind of glad, in a way; David was so bad I couldn't help but look good.

The actual process of shooting a scene is nothing like I imagined. We have to do it over and over for each camera angle, then the editors paste it all together. In between, the location make-up lady, Gwenda, touches up our faces and hair. There is so much spray in mine that I feel like I have a slab of concrete on my head!

The crew is never ending, though I have no idea what

any of them actually do. I had one scene with Norma, who was in a grizzly mood. She kept complaining about her dialogue and changing it as we were shooting. As a result, I kept on missing my cues. The director, Simon Manson, had a go at her.

The shoot ended at around six, then I had to see Flora again and go through my scenes for tomorrow. At least I have the amendments, so I won't be taken by surprise. I have no energy left to write, but somehow I must go over my lines again. Help!

December 1

7.30p.m.   Mosman Manor

I've survived another day. I was at a different location – the outside of Sasha's apartment. I had three scenes with Norton, I mean David, but one of them got cut so that made life a little easier. David isn't unpleasant, he's just not my idea of a switched-on guy. He talks at me, rather than to me. At the moment I feel like killing him.

Simon didn't say all that much, though I got the feeling he didn't care what I did. He just wanted to do the job and get out of there. The crew are much the same. The only time they smile is at lunch. There is so much food! Puff pastry, cream cakes. I didn't eat a thing. I'm so proud of myself! I have location again tomorrow. We're shooting at a car dealer's. Sasha is buying a car!

December 2

My third day on the job – I feel like I've been doing it forever! I only had one scene today, which allowed me more time to observe the cast and the crew. The assistant director, Steve, has become my first friend on the show. His job, as the title suggests, is to assist the director. There are four different directors on the show, who rotate from week to week. Steve told me this often makes it difficult for the actors, who have to keep changing their performance to support the individual director. I also got to know Gwenda, the make-up lady. She's quite bitter and twisted – seems like a common trait among the crew. She complained about having to work really long hours and always getting into trouble from Casper, whom she's nicknamed the 'seducer producer'. She told me to watch out for him.

December 3

I had an awful day on location. We were shooting at Cronulla Beach and the weather was hot and windy. Every time I said a line I'd end up with a mouthful of sand! On top of this, there was a crowd of onlookers poised with their cameras. Though it felt exciting to be the centre of attention, I felt very nervous. To make matters worse,

David continued to botch his lines. This is the first time I've seen Simon lose his temper. David felt terrible. Poor guy, he obviously has trouble learning his lines. Next week will be more nerve-wracking, with my first session in the studio. Thank God tomorrow is Saturday. I have two days to work myself up to it.

December 4

8.35p.m.   Mosman Manor

I can't believe it is a Saturday night and I am snuggled up in bed about to go to sleep. I have had such an exhausting week that I've no energy to go out.

I had lunch with Nadine today, which was quite unusual. She's happy about my job on *Mercy Hospital*, but not about other things: Troy. I told her I regret what has happened. I even admitted I wish we hadn't broken up. Nadine said nothing, keeping her opinion to herself. The afternoon disappeared without any of the usual jokes or jibes, just flat conversation. It's as though we were never good friends.

I got home to find a long list of house-cleaning chores from Mum. I have hardly been home the last few days so haven't had a chance to do anything, now she expects me to catch up on the washing and dusting! I had a huge argument with her. Dad chipped in, saying just because I am a television star doesn't mean I can neglect my responsibilities at home. All I had wanted to do was to have a pleasant conversation, find out all the family news and restore some normality to my chaotic life. I guess I was asking too much.

December 5

I feel like Cinderella. I spent the entire day catching up on the housework, which also included cleaning the pool and sweeping the driveway. I only agreed because the sun was out so I could get a tan at the same time. I thought a lot about work, about the family and about Troy. I haven't got my priorities right. The show should be number one, yet everything else is getting in the way. I have my first day in the studio tomorrow. We rehearse half the studio scenes on a Monday, then tape them on Tuesday. We rehearse again on Wednesday, then tape Thursday and Friday. I should be mentally prepared, yet my mind is sidetracked by all these other trivial matters. I will have a lot to tell you tomorrow night.

December 6

9.15p.m.   *Mosman Manor*

My first day in studio! I mumbled my way through rehearsal, doing my best to follow Flora's instructions and listen to Simon, the director. They have completely opposing ideas on how to play the scenes.

I met some of the other cast. Desiree, who plays Sarah,

welcomed me with open arms. I thought she was really nice until Bradley Hart, who plays Cliff, told me to watch out for her. I thought he was nice until Angie Purcell, who plays Veronica, told me Brad was a sleaze bag. Apparently they had a bit of a fling, but it's all over now. I can't believe how bitchy the place is! They all worked so fast. Brad, who has been on the show for years, didn't listen to anything Simon said. He played all the scenes the way he wanted to. Angie, too, had ideas of her own but Simon exercised some control over her. Desiree is actually the best actress of all of them.

December 7

11.15p.m.   Mosman Manor

Lights, camera . . . would Melanie please stop blocking this shot! That just about sums up today, my first taping in the studio. It was nothing like I imagined. I reported for make-up at six-thirty a.m. Billy, the studio make-up artist, is really nice. He had a dig at Juanita Philips. Bad back – I bet! Billy claims it's just an excuse to cover up her regular visits to the plastic surgeon. If she has got a bad back, it's because she's carrying that extra silicone!

I was supposed to shoot my first scene at seven, but Norma was having another fit in the studio so I didn't start until eight. I was glad, as I got to sit in the 'green room' (the actors' waiting room) and chat to some of the other cast. The more I talk to Desiree the more I like her.

Then, it was my turn. I made plenty of mistakes – missing my mark, tripping over the cables and standing out of frame. But it was my first day, for heaven's sake! All Simon's direction comes via Steve as Simon isn't actually on set during taping. He's just a voice from the control room. The crew call him God.

The studio crew are much worse than the location crew. Desiree says it's because they never see the light of day. They are overworked and underpaid. I think they are the laziest, most uncouth bunch of slobs I have seen in my life.

Then there are all these people running around, checking sets and making notes. I don't know what they do, but today I felt superior – as though they were fussing about for me! When I was on the monitor, I was the most important person. There again, when I stuffed up every eye was on me as well!

December 8

10.45p.m.   Mosman Manor

I'm going to bed. I'm so tired I hope I sleep for a thousand years.

December 9

6.30p.m.   Channel Five

I'm sitting in the green room. I have one more scene to go, scripts coming out of my ears . . . I need a break! This

morning began with a photo shoot. The new look cast of
Mercy Hospital, as well as individual shots of myself and
David. Once again, Jerry took the shots. I had an hour off
after the shoot so I shouted Jerry a coffee in the canteen.
I told him about my situation at home. I told him about
breaking up with Troy, how Mosman was full of painful
memories and that I needed to make a clean break. He
really understood. Truly. He suggested I move out, make
a fresh start. So happens, he has a spare room going in
his apartment. The rent is cheap, plenty of space. The
apartment is in Kings Cross, but the building is new and
there is plenty of security. He lives with some other guy,
Kent. He's also an entertainer. Jerry suggested I think
about it, and if I'm interested, come over and have a look.
But I'm not ready to move out of home . . . not yet.

December 10

5.00p.m.   Channel Five

Norma Applegate is making my life hell. For years I have
watched her on *Mercy Hospital*, imagining she was a nice,
caring, considerate woman like her character. I thought
we'd get along well. Boy was I wrong. She is tempera-
mental, childish and inconsiderate and hates the whole
concept of my character on the show. She gives me no
help or support and she makes me nervous. I knew all my
lines when I went into work this morning, but the minute
I saw Norma I forgot them. We had to rehearse the scene

where Sasha tells her she is her daughter. Flora and I had worked for hours on the scene, trying to get the emotional level just right. Norma, however, plays her lines with such anger I can't help losing my temper. If this is going to happen in all our scenes together, I don't know how I will cope. Thank God tomorrow is Saturday. I'm not going to worry about a thing all day.

December 11 & 12

6.45p.m.   *Mosman Jetty*

The weekend has disappeared. I haven't gone out, seen anybody or done a thing. I've spent every waking hour learning lines or thinking about the show. This is the true meaning of dedication. I do feel bad about not having time to see my friends. Voni and Karen have both left several messages at home, but I don't have the energy to see them. I know what they will ask: 'What is he like? What is she like? What happens when . . .?' I just can't handle it. Strangely, the only person I have called is Nadine. But she hasn't called me back. I think she is still angry at me for neglecting Troy, but the fact still remains . . . he dumped me! I'm the one who deserves her sympathy!

December 13

Now I know why Gwenda calls Casper the seducer producer. Slobbering on a fat cigar, he came into the green room this afternoon. He knew full well I was on my own. He said he was on a routine tour of the studio, just checking on things and making sure everyone was OK. He had such a lecherous look about him and he's *so* unattractive – overweight or what? My stomach turns just thinking about it! I told him I was fine. Thankfully, rehearsals were running ahead of schedule so he didn't get as much time with me as he probably hoped he would. What am I going to do?

December 14

4.00p.m.   *Botany Bay Hospital*

This is the first time since I started in the show I have actually been bored. We're shooting an ambulance sequence. I don't have much dialogue, but I am stuck here for the three hour shoot. The only exciting thing that has happened is some kids asking for my autograph.

Though Sasha isn't on screen yet, people who watch the taping say I am going to be a huge star! David is on his way over. I can't wait for his latest instalment of meaningless conversation. I'd better put you away.

December 15

I have a big problem on my hands. Casper made a pass at me! I thought I was overreacting, but later investigation leaves no doubt – this was a pass. He invited me on his private yacht for the weekend. He said his wife was out of town and his children were staying with friends. He said he wanted to talk about future storylines, help me with my performance. I politely declined, which he interpreted as 'some other time'. The man is such a lech!

December 16

I have a very busy schedule. Most of my scenes are with Norma and David, so I need this breather to recharge my batteries. I talked to Sue-Ellen today. Without mentioning names or details, I outlined my problem with Casper. Sue-Ellen was concerned, but I got the distinct feeling she is loathe to do anything about it. If I make a complaint I may jeopardise my job – whether the complaint is founded or not. Her advice for the time being is to avoid the person at all costs. I get the feeling she has heard this gripe before and, from experience, knows this is the best way to deal with it. I'm not so sure. Every time I see Casper I get a shiver down my spine. I certainly can't avoid him given he is the producer of the show, but I shouldn't have to put up with this either. I can't believe my dream job is turning into such a nightmare!

December 17

9.00p.m.   *Channel Five*

Just my luck. It is the last day of the week and I am in the first scene and the last. I started out in the studio then had to go to location, then back to studio again this evening. I have had so many wardrobe changes I feel like a mannequin!

I had a surprise visitor this morning – Mum! She has been nagging me for weeks to let her come on set, but I've been stalling her for a very good reason. My fears were confirmed – it was the most embarrassing experience of my life! Mum kept showing me up in front of the other actors, talking about my childhood and how I always was an attention seeker. I wanted to die then and there! I think I'll go and visit Nadine tomorrow. I'm sure she'll cheer me up.

December 18

7.45p.m.   *Mosman Manor*

Words cannot describe the shock, anger and confusion I feel. I have just had a coffee with Nadine. She told me she and Troy kissed! I nearly died. How could this be happening? Has this been going on before my very eyes?

Nadine insists it all happened accidentally. Troy has been upset since we split up. Nadine has been comforting him. Somehow, some way . . . it just happened. I know Troy and I have split. I shouldn't care any more. But I still have a lot of feeling for Troy, and Nadine is – or was – my best friend. Nadine plans to back right off. She doesn't want this to come between our friendship, yet she felt I had a right to know. I didn't know what to say. I don't know what to do . . . only that I have to get out of here.

December 19

1.30p.m.   Sydney Harbour

I'm on the ferry, on my way back from looking at Jerry's apartment. I had remembered him saying he had a room to rent. I know this must seem impulsive, but I woke up this morning and found the answer to my problem: leave home; away from the stress of Mum and Dad, Nadine and Troy.

The spare room has a great view of the city. Kent, Jerry's flatmate, wasn't there, but his room was tidy so I take that as a good sign. All things considered, it is perfect for me. The next crossroad is the big intersection: telling Mum and Dad. It will have to be tonight. Wish me luck.

7.30p.m.   Mosman Manor

Mum and Dad are furious. They say I'm too young to move out of home, least of all with two guys I hardly know. And to Kings Cross! I tried to pretend that the postal

54

address was Elizabeth Bay, a more respectable suburb, but it didn't wash. Anyway, I have made up my mind. For all the reasons I have said too many times, I need to move. I'll stay until Christmas, but then I'm gone. My relationship with my parents is in turmoil, I have drifted away from most of my old friends and I'm not giving my career the attention it deserves. So it's time to make a resolution: a new year, a new home, a new start.

December 20

8.45p.m.   *Mosman Manor*

Telephone, telegraph . . . tell Billy! I made the mistake of telling Billy about my plans to move in with Jerry and, by the end of the day, every person on the show knew about it. Norma made an acidic remark about me climbing my way to the top as if the only reason I was moving in with Jerry was to further my career. That skinny, balding Brad made some comment along the lines of, Melanie is going to become another of Jerry's conquests. Who does he think he is? A comment about his receding hairline soon put him in his place! Desiree was the only one who gave me the benefit of the doubt, though she did give me a friendly warning. Jerry does have a lot of girlfriends and he may be planning to make me one of them. Desiree thinks I'm sensible enough to take care of myself, but am I? I thought Jerry was such a nice guy. What have I let myself in for?

December 21

It's beginning to feel a lot like Christmas. The show isn't having a production break, despite the fact it goes off air for several weeks. There have been a lot of complaints from the cast and crew but there really is nothing they can do about it. We are all contracted to work. I'm actually quite happy. Although I'm exhausted, the work is still fresh and stimulating.

I came face to face with Casper today, the first encounter since he made the pass at me. He heard I'm moving in with Jerry which is good and bad. Good because he is backing off, but bad because the reason is he assumes Jerry and I are now on together. Why does everyone think this?

December 22

10.00p.m.   *Channel Five*

I can't believe I am still at the studio. There are scheduling problems so, as a result, I'm running late. All my scenes have been with David. Excruciating! I had a session with Flora this afternoon. We worked through a scene where Sasha blows her top. I drew on all the negative energy I am feeling at home and turned it into a positive, powerhouse performance! I really feel as though this is the essence of acting – being able to draw on real life experiences and apply them to a character. Every time I do a scene I try to match Sasha's emotion with a real situation in which I have felt the same way. The strategy seems to be working. I have to go – I think I'm on.

December 23

9.35p.m.   *Mosman Manor*

I have to save all my energy for tomorrow night. The Channel Five Christmas Party! Tell you all about it.

December 24

11.50p.m.   *Mosman Manor*

I've just looked at my watch and realised it's almost Christmas Day! How time flies when you're having fun! I don't know where to begin. The Channel Five Christmas Party was a scream. It was at a restaurant overlooking the harbour, though the only view I got was of famous faces laughing, dancing and tripping from one side of the room to the other. I could write pages about that, but there is something much more important I want to say – I have met the man of my dreams. Well, I think so. His name is Danny. I don't know how to describe him. He's got brown hair and incredible blue eyes. I guess he's good-looking in a non-conventional kind of way. He's not that tall – but what a body! Wow! He has an infectious personality, yet he is quiet and unassuming.

I guess he's a mystery – and I want to solve him!

We met on the dance floor. Danny organised the music for the night, a blend of funk, soul and dance. He whisked me off to a table and we talked for hours. He seemed genuinely interested in me. Come to think of it, I didn't find out much about him. Every time our conversation turned in his direction, he'd find a way to flip it back on to me. Then there was a problem with the music so he left to sort it out. I spent the last couple of hours looking for him, but he was nowhere to be found.

I feel like Prince Charming, though I don't even have a glass slipper. Next week I'm on a mission. I want that man!

December 25

7.55p.m.   Mosman Manor

Christmas Day. I feel like I have eaten an entire turkey which has somehow come back to life in my stomach and is trying to fight its way out. Christmas lunch was at Auntie Roberta's, the typical family gathering. All my cousins went crazy, demanding my autograph and asking when I come on air. The last time I saw them they hated my guts. Now, all of a sudden, they are my best friends. I got pretty sick of it all by late afternoon, so was relieved when Dad finally gave the nod for us to head home.

Christmas Dinner was a smaller affair, just the four of us. There was an unmistakable tension, clearly because I am moving out tomorrow. After dinner, I made the traditional trip to Troy's house. Normally I would have gone over for dinner but since we've broken up, I decided a short but sweet visit would be more appropriate. I bought him the wetsuit he's wanted for ages. Before *Mercy Hospital* I didn't think I'd ever be able to afford to buy it, but now I'm on good money and he is worth the expense. The situation was all very awkward, especially since he knew that I knew what had happened with Nadine, though neither of us mentioned it. Nadine has gone away with her family, so I haven't seen her at all. This is a good thing as I don't know what I would say if she were around. I'm glad I'm moving out tomorrow. I won't have to think about it at all.

December 26

7.40p.m.   Jerry's Junk-yard

You really know who your friends are when you have to move house in a taxi. Mum and Dad refused to help, of course, and Karen, Shane and Voni all had plans they couldn't cancel. I was half tempted to call on Troy and his pizza delivery-van, but pride prevented me. So I piled all my stuff into a water cab and zipped across the harbour.

Three trips back and forth and I am happily settled at 'Jerry's Junk-yard'. I think. I have just met Kent, the other guy who lives here. He's very quiet. A bit of a bookworm. I tried to strike up a conversation, asking him what kind of entertainer he was. He didn't reply. I can hear Abba music coming out of his bedroom!

Jerry is out with some girl. I think she's a model. I made it clear I wanted to keep our relationship strictly platonic, which he happily accepted. All I can think about is Danny, the guy I met at the Christmas party. I know it sounds strange, but I think I've met him somewhere before. I'm not sure why it didn't strike me at the time, but now I realise his face is familiar. I'll have to stop thinking about it. It's driving me crazy!

December 27

8.45p.m.   Channel Five

I'm sitting in the green room, trying to keep my eyes open. It has been a long day, fraught with problems and delays. Brad caught too much sun over the break so make-up has to pale his skin. This adds another ten minutes to every scene he is in. Norma complained about a couple of scenes – both with my character – so they had to be rewritten causing another setback. Also, someone broke into the studio and stole some medical equipment. Now all the operating theatre scenes are postponed until later in the week, by which time they will have recovered the equipment or bought new stuff. For all these reasons I have found it hard to turn in a good performance, and, on top of all this, we have a new director, some guy named Aldov Sitzen. Apparently he's directed feature films but has hit hard times and is now doing soaps. He wants to turn everything into a big screen adventure. And, in his own words, I am 'small screen material'. I think somebody should remind him this *is* the small screen!

Despite all this, my mind is elsewhere. Danny . . . now where have I seen him before?

December 28

10.45p.m.   Jerry's Junk-yard

The mystery is solved! I know exactly where I have seen Danny. It all came together on the way home as my cab was driving down Oxford Street. I was looking at all the clubs (fantasising about finally being able to get into them), when I saw PMT. Bingo. Remember last month the girls and I couldn't get in? There was a guy, standing in the doorway, staring at me. I couldn't put my finger on it at the time. I didn't know who he was, or why he was paying me such attention, but there was something about him . . . That guy was Danny! Maybe he is a DJ there? Anyway, he knows who I am and what I do. If he really likes me he'll find me. Do you think he likes me? We spent hours talking at the Christmas party. He didn't care about all the other stars, he cared about me. I hope he calls . . .

December 29

3.30p.m.   Tarronga Zoo

Believe it or not, I am surrounded by elephants, lions and chimpanzees! I am on location at the zoo. The storyline is completely over the top. Vince and Sasha are at the zoo having their first romantic day out. One of the giraffes gets trapped trying to escape its enclosure and the vet is trampled in the process. Then it's Doctor Vince and Nurse Sasha to the rescue! I'm finding it hard to take any of this seriously, but as Flora says, 'if it's in the script, make it happen'.

Anyway, the stunt doubles have taken over and I have a couple of hours to sit around and do nothing. I really should pop home and see Mum and Dad. Mosman Manor is just round the corner. I have spoken to them a couple of times since I moved; their tone has been icy. I know they are waiting for me to fall flat on my face. Although I miss them, it's probably a good idea for me to keep my distance. What is it they say? Absence makes the heart grow fonder? Yes, some time apart will do us all the world of good.

December 30

11.00p.m.   Jerry's Junk-yard

The last few days have been hectic. I could go on for hours about the show, but there's something much more important I want to tell you: I have heard from Danny. He sent me a *personal* invitation to PMT's exclusive New Year's Eve party! (None of the other cast got invited.) There was a message: 'Hope you can make it.' This means he likes me, right? He wouldn't invite me otherwise, right?

December 31

5.45p.m.   Channel Five

I'm still at the studio, with three more scenes to go. I can't wait for tonight. I have heard lots of the other cast talking about the PMT party, complaining that they have not been invited. I also heard Angie mention Danny's name. Apparently, he is very important at the club. I'm going to have the time of my life.

January 1

10.35p.m.   Jerry's Junk-yard

The last twenty-four hours have formed the best day of my life. OK, maybe not the best. But I have had a great time. The PMT party was wild. Danny met me at the door and led me off to the upstairs bar. He set me up with drinks for the night. I wanted to ask him a thousand questions, but my heart was beating like a drum and I was so overcome by the whole experience I could hardly speak. Then he disappeared. I spent the next couple of hours chatting to some really interesting people. I felt more comfortable asking them the questions. Boy did I get some answers! Danny is not a DJ: his step-father, C.D. Greenwood, *owns* PMT! And a few other nightclubs and bars.

Just before midnight, Danny reappeared. He apologised and said he'd had a few business matters to take care of, but for the rest of the night he was mine. We counted in the new year together. On the stroke of midnight he kissed me. Not a long, lingering tongue dive. His lips kind of caressed mine, giving me just a taste then leaving me hanging for more. Danny is the first guy I've kissed since Troy, only the fifth guy I've kissed in my life. I've never felt like that with anyone before.

The rest of the night fell somewhere between agony and ecstasy as I struggled to work out what Danny wanted from me. I'm not even sure I know what I want from him. We danced for the rest of the night. He didn't say much when the cab dropped me home this morning, just 'see you around'. I have spent most of today in bed, wondering what my next move will be. Danny took the initiative by inviting me last night; the next advance has to be mine.

January 2

7.30p.m.   Jerry's Junk-yard

I couldn't put it off any longer. I've been avoiding them for a week, but today I finally bit the bullet and made an appearance at home. Mum and Dad reinforced their disapproval of my absence, this time replacing anger with emotional blackmail. Dad is genuinely hurt. He feels as though he can't provide for his own daughter and, now that I have hit the big time, I am turning my back on them. Mum, too, is deeply upset. This is the first time I've actually considered their true feelings. Before it's all been screaming and shouting; I now realise there is real emotion involved. I tried to tell them it's not anything they have said or done, but that I'm growing up. I need to spread my wings and find my own way in the world.

I was beginning to consider moving back home, but Sebastian's newsflash put an end to that idea. He said he saw Troy and Nadine together at the local shops. They looked very 'friendly'. A couple of days later he saw Troy's pizza delivery-van parked outside Nadine's house. So much for Nadine's promise to back off. My ex-boyfriend and my best friend are now a couple! Well, this only gives me more motivation to make a go of my new life. There is no turning back.

January 3

8.30p.m.   Channel Five

My horoscope said my day would be filled with 'romantic surprises, pressure at work and sudden notoriety'. That pretty much describes my day. The romantic surprise came from Danny – a dozen red roses delivered to the studio. The note read 'Looking forward to seeing more of you in the new year'.

I had a smile on my face until rehearsal got underway. Norma threw a massive tantrum in the middle of a scene, complaining that the storyline was totally implausible and she wasn't going to act it any more. This week's director gave her a severe dressing down in front of everyone. This prompted Norma to march right out of the studio and into Casper's office. She didn't reappear all day, but rumour has it her contract is up for renewal and she may not be re-signing. I'm really worried about what this means for me. I know I've just started a six-month contract, but if my on-screen mother leaves the show what will be left for my character? I thought a lot about this until I saw the latest issue of *Exclusive* – the sudden notoriety my horoscope predicted. They ran a double spread on David and me, describing us as the hot new couple on *Mercy Hospital*. I can't believe it! My first episode hasn't even gone on air.

I have one more scene to rehearse – with David – then I'm planning a romantic surprise of my own.

10.50p.m.   Jerry's Junk-yard

My surprise has backfired. I stopped by PMT on the way home, hoping to catch Danny and thank him for the flowers. I saw him, but he was in the weirdest mood. He wasn't happy to see me, nor did he take the time to chat. He said he was busy and would call me tomorrow. I don't get it. Why has he turned cold on me?

January 4

I'm about to drop dead any minute. Today has been non-stop. The only thing that didn't happen was a phone call from Danny. I have a horrible feeling it's all over. I shouldn't have gone to PMT last night. I shouldn't have bothered him.

January 5

8.45p.m.   Channel Five

I swear I live my life in this studio – I still have a couple more scenes to go. But I mustn't wish it away. Already I feel the credits rolling on Sasha, because Norma Applegate is leaving the show. No, she didn't quit; according to Steve, Norma has had to leave because of 'irreconcilable differences' – I don't think! I don't really care if she gets hit by a bus; all I care about is the fact Sasha no longer has a mother – and possibly no place in *Mercy Hospital*. I talked to one of the writers – I always forget his name, is it Ron? Ross? Roger? – anyway, what's-his-name said they haven't decided what to do with Sasha. In other words, they are going to write her out but don't want to tell me until the last minute! Billy confirmed this is the usual procedure. If someone is getting dropped, Casper waits until the last possible second to tell them, so they have less time to play up and generate bad press.

On top of this, Danny still hasn't called. And, for some inexplicable reason, this morning half my washing had disappeared from the line. I think I will hang myself from it when I get home.

January 6

5.00p.m.   Channel Five

Life has taken a turn for the better. Danny called! Well, I didn't speak to him personally but the production secretary took a message. He has my mobile number and is going to phone me later on. Crisis: what if he wants to tell me it's all over? Wait a minute, what is there to be over? I mean, we haven't really done anything yet. He couldn't possibly call it quits at this early stage of the game. In any case, I haven't got time to think about it. Today is stress city. Now that Norma is leaving, she is going out of her way to make life a misery for all of us. She changes every line, so I always miss my cue. I wish I knew why she doesn't like me. Desiree said Norma doesn't like any of the young cast because she doesn't consider them serious actors. Norma started out as a film actress, but now she's stuck on a cardboard set pretending to perform operations with a pound of sausages and a bottle of tomato sauce. I guess she's bitter.

At least David is improving. Flora has spent a lot of time coaching him and he is showing a few signs of life. I shouldn't be too hard on the guy. He means well, but a kind heart does not make him an actor.

Here I am, sounding like I've been doing it for years! In all honesty, I'm happy with my performance. I think everyone is.

10.45p.m.   Jerry's Junk-yard

I have been sitting on the edge of my seat for hours. Finally, Danny called. He apologised for being rude to me at PMT the other night. He said he was under a lot of pressure with work, but everything has calmed down. He invited me to a launch at PMT on Saturday night, then suggested that we go out afterwards. This time I'm going to make *him* sweat. I simply said I'd get back to him. I will accept, of course, but two can play this game. If he's going to play hard to get, I'm going to play impossible.

January 7

10.35p.m.   Jerry's Junk-yard

I'm having an early night. Today was no more stressful than yesterday. If only viewers knew what went on behind the scenes! Norma's behaviour has put several noses out of joint. Billy – my number one source of gossip – tells me a few other contracts are up for renewal and a lot of the cast are thinking about leaving. This is good news for me as they will want to keep all the new characters to fill the gaps. Also, the *Sydney Observer* ran an article on David and I. They basically said the same as *Exclusive* magazine, but hinted we were a breath of fresh air – just what the show needs. I saw Bradley Hart reading it at lunch-time. He didn't look too happy. He's had quite a lot of bad publicity lately, especially after he was spotted coming out of a sex shop. I can't quite work him out. I guess he's had a bad childhood. Maybe he's just been on the show too long; three years in this place and I'd be punching walls.

On a better note, I phoned Danny and told him I'd meet him at PMT tomorrow night. I'm looking forward to it, but this on-one-minute-off-the-next business is driving me crazy. Have we got something going or not?

January 8 & 9

3.40p.m.   Jerry's Junk-yard

Buckle your seat-belt, I have a lot to tell you! I met Danny at PMT last night. The place was pumping. Head Injuries, a dance band, launched their new single. It's called 'Melt Your Body', exactly what Danny did to me. I'm crazy about him! He stayed by my side the entire night, making sure no other guy had a chance. We danced for hours, then popped into Hot Lips – that's right, the drag club! We caught the last show. After a Madonna impersonator, a Kylie lookalike and more gay men than my hairdressing salon, Kitty Kat came out on stage. As she pelted out 'Dancing Queen', I knew there was something familiar about her, er, him. The dress, the make-up . . . it was mine. And the man behind the woman was Kent, my flatmate!

That's right, Kent is a drag queen! My eyes popped out of my head. Suddenly it all made sense. The Abba music coming out of his bedroom, my clothes disappearing from the line . . . Kent has been leading a double life! All this time I thought he was some mild-mannered cabaret singer, now I find out he is Priscilla, Queen of the Desert! Danny could tell I was uneasy so he whisked me out of there. I wasn't sure why we went in the first place. Truth be known, I was a little worried about his sexuality. Danny, however, explained it perfectly. He said he was open-minded, tolerant of all beliefs and sexualities. And the shows *are* fantastic.

Before we knew it, the time was four in the morning. I invited him home for a coffee. Kent was in bed, Jerry with his girlfriend – a different one. Anyway, we sat and talked. The next thing I remember is waking up in his arms. On the couch, of course. Nothing happened, but I felt the most amazing afterglow.

Kent disappeared soon after breakfast. I couldn't say anything to him about last night. I have nothing against his career but I wish he'd wear his own clothes! Danny and I were going to spend today at Bondi, but a stack of scripts arrived on my doorstep. Rewrites for next week. Apparently Norma is 'sick', so the writers have pulled her out for a few shows. I really wanted to spend the day with Danny, but he insisted work come first. So, on my front doorstep, he walked out of my life again. I'm sure he will be back.

January 10

Today has been a total nightmare. Norma's mystery illness has thrown the show into chaos. All my scenes are now with the most unlikely people, simply because it couldn't be any other way. I now understand why things sometimes look out of place on television, why characters tell other characters things they wouldn't naturally tell. It has nothing to do with the writers losing the plot. There are so many external factors involved, factors an audience can't possibly appreciate.

I have to get some sleep. Later.

January 11

10.30p.m.   *Jerry's Junk-yard*

I'm about to collapse. The past couple of days have been so busy I haven't had the chance to think about Danny, which is just as well as he hasn't called. On the home front, 'Melrose Place' (my nickname for this madhouse!) is starting to get on my nerves. Jerry has yet another girlfriend. I think her name is Cindy. His room is down the hall, yet I can hear them giggling and carrying on from here. Then, on the other side of the junk-yard, I can hear Kent practising his moves. I really liked Abba before I moved in, but if I hear 'Money, Money, Money' one more time I'll punch the wall! Wait here,

I'm going to tell them to keep the noise down.

11.00p.m.

Maybe I shouldn't have done that. I kept banging on Jerry's door, but there was no answer so I barged in and found a startled Jerry with Cindy. Cindy screamed! I've never felt so embarrassed in my life. Jerry told me to get the hell outta there, which is exactly what I did.

Back in my room, I got all high and mighty and decided to pay Kent a visit. I didn't even bother to knock. I caught him parading round in another one of my dresses – the wild card from the Miss Bondi contest. I told him to take it off, wash it and never borrow my clothes again! What's more, I told him to practise his act somewhere else. I feel much better now.

January 12

4.35p.m.   Channel Five

I'm sitting in the make-up room. Billy is putting the final touch to Juanita's face – yes, her back is *fine*.

Danny phoned to ask me out to dinner tonight. I'm working late so I can't. He then suggested tomorrow night, but it's my first night on air and I promised to go to Mum and Dad's so we could watch it together. The night after we will finally get together.

I talked to the writer, this afternoon. He assured me Sasha is definitely staying with the show, which is one good thing. While I was waiting in his office I snuck a look at some forward planning notes. Apparently Sasha and Vince are getting engaged! This means that I will have to do thousands more scenes with David!

January 13

10.00p.m.   Jerry's Junk-yard

Tonight was the night. Seven p.m. in households around Australia, Sasha Somers hit the screen. I watched my very first episode at Mosman Manor with Mum, Dad and Sebastian. I was so nervous. I had seen the rushes – the unedited playbacks of new material – but not the entire cut, so it was all pretty new to me. My first scene was the one where Sasha gets bowled over by the horse. I had to pinch myself when I came on screen. This is something I've been dreaming about for years and now, it's finally happened. I looked so fat! Other than that, I thought I was pretty good.

The half hour seemed to fly. Mum and Dad smiled, pride gleaming in their eyes. This is the first ceasefire we have had since I moved out. Dad admitted he had underestimated me. Seeing me on screen, in front of the nation, he now realises that I have grown up. It felt so good to hear him say that.

Thereafter, the home phone and my mobile haven't stopped ringing. Most of the calls were from Sebastian's friends wanting my autograph, but there was an important one for me. Troy. He asked if he could come over and talk. So he did and we did. Troy had watched the episode at home. It had made him realise how much he missed me in his life. We didn't talk about Nadine, or the possibility that we could get back together again, just that we should stay friends. I agreed. Now as I lie in my bed, I wonder if I even want to be friends. I still have feelings for Troy. Even though Danny has replaced him in my life, they are different people and my feelings for them are not the same. All things considered, Danny is where my future is. Troy is a phase in my life that's over, so maybe it's best to leave it at that?

January 14

5.35p.m.   Jerry's Junk-yard

My hand is killing me! I've been signing autographs. I had the entire afternoon off so decided to go grocery shopping. Big mistake. All the school kids were on their way home and recognised me. They screamed 'Sasha! Sasha! Sasha!' I had to sign my name on their school bags, text books, plaster casts . . . you name it. I even had to catch a cab home as I was scared they would follow me.

Back home, I discovered the most expensive bottle of champagne I have ever seen. The note from Danny read 'Congratulations on your performance last night. I can't wait to see you live in person tonight.' He's sending a cab at eight!

11.30p.m.   Jerry's Junk-yard

Tonight was great. Danny and I had dinner in the revolving
restaurant of the Centrepoint Tower. Danny said he
wanted me to see just how many people were watching
me – the view covers the whole of Sydney! I told him
about my new-found fame, how it's like a dream come
true – yet I don't know how he fits into it. Danny said he
fits in whatever way I want him to. He really likes me and
wants us to spend more time together. However, he
doesn't want to pressure me or come on too strong. I
said I wanted to know more about him, enter his world
the way he enters mine. He assured me this would happen,
with time. The clock is ticking . . .

January 15

7.45p.m.   Channel Five

The workload is never-ending. I thought I'd be out of
here by a decent hour, but the scenes keep coming.
Tamara, the publicist, hauled David and I into her office
today. Apparently there have been a lot of publicity
requests for us: magazines, talk shows, shopping centre
appearances. Tamara believes David and I have the chance
to become the next super couple, the biggest draw on the
show. She made a very interesting suggestion. I can't quite
remember how she put it, the bottom line is she wants
David and I to pretend we are a real life couple. Tamara
believes the publicity advantages would be enormous, à la

Jason and Kylie. David and I sat there, jaws dropping. Pretend we are a real life couple, as in going out together? Tamara nodded. She didn't pressure us for a response. Instead, she suggested we think it over.

David and I walked out together, unsure of what to think. David has a girlfriend, Marianne, and I have Danny. What would they think? How could we possibly pull it off?

January 16

8.30p.m.   *High in the sky*

I am on a plane, destined for Perth. Brad and Angie pulled out of a publicity appearance, so Tamara substituted David and me. We are doing a telethon and shopping centre guest spot, which could be a lot of fun. The flight is three hours. David has spent the first hour in the toilet. He's feeling really sick. I think I can hear him coming back now, so I'll put this away.

January 17

1.00p.m.   *Perth*

I'm lucky to be alive. David and I did the appearance at the shopping centre. I'm not sure what suburb it was in. I've never experienced anything like it – kids screaming our names, holding out their hands for an autograph, or at the very least a touch. We have only been on screen a few nights, yet they have read every article about us and know every intimate detail. At one point we had to answer questions from the audience. Everyone asked us if we were a real life couple! I couldn't believe it! We both blushed, unsure of what to say in the light of Tamara's suggestion. They jumped to the conclusion that there was something going on, but we were too embarrassed to admit it. Before we had a chance to deny anything we were whisked into a limousine and dumped back at the hotel.

I'm now in my five star suite, relaxing in the spa. David is next door. We have to be at Perth Channel Five in a couple of hours, where we will appear in the telethon and take calls from donors.

January 18

6.35p.m.   High in the sky

The most romantic thing happened to me last night. I was taking donations from viewers when I got a call from some guy named Wilbur. He said he'd donate one thousand dollars to the telethon if I met him after the show. I didn't know what to do, but because it was for a worthy cause (the children's hospital), I decided it would do no harm especially if I could persuade David to accompany me. After all, Wilbur only wanted to meet me back at my hotel and buy me a drink. David agreed to come. As we walked into the lobby, who should we see but Danny, alias Wilbur! He had flown all the way from Sydney to be with me! I was so thrilled to see him. The next surprise came when he escorted me outside. A horse–drawn carriage awaited. Danny had organised a midnight tour of Perth, complete with champagne. I have never felt so special in my life. The tour lasted until four in the morning, by which time we were both exhausted. We crashed in my hotel room. Again, nothing happened. I thought Danny would make a move on me, but because I didn't make any advance on him, he held back. It's not that I didn't want to. I did. The timing was perfect. But I was tired.

Danny took an early flight home this morning, while David and I did another appearance. Once again there were people everywhere, shouting and screaming our names. This weekend has been amazing.

January 19

8.45p.m.   Jerry's Junk-yard

Another long day. Norma has made a miraculous recovery and is now back at work so things have calmed down. Tamara showed David and I a report from a Perth newspaper, all about the shopping centre appearances. We are pictured together, underneath the headline, 'Real Life Lovers?' Tamara used this as justification for us to go through with the real life romance ruse. I'm not so sure. I have Danny to consider, the man of my dreams.

I left a message at PMT (I still don't have his home phone number), thanking Danny for a great weekend. He hasn't phoned back. I'm too tired to talk to him anyway.

January 20

9.00p.m.   Jerry's Junk-yard

The situation is getting out of hand. Kent has his Abba music playing full blast. He knows that I know about his secret life as a drag queen, and is now unabashed about rehearsing. Jerry has yet another girl. The man is the biggest slut I have ever met! I thought it would be really cool living with him, that we'd have really deep conversations and hang out together. But all he does is work and sleep with different women. I'm afraid the honeymoon is over. I can't take much more of this.

January 21

10.45p.m.   Jerry's Junk-yard

I just fell in the door, literally. Danny and I have been out to dinner but I was so tired I kept nodding off at the table. My workload is just ridiculous. My scenes are scheduled far apart, but there is no point zipping home during the breaks. I end up spending eighteen hour days in the green room, waiting for my turn and watching everyone else open fan mail.

On the bright side, dinner – the part I was awake for –

was wonderful. Danny listened to all my problems on the home front. He suggested I have a long talk with Jerry and Kent and, if the situation doesn't improve, move out to a place on my own. The last suggestion makes a lot of sense. I can afford to move, that wouldn't be an issue. And Kings Cross is hardly a safe place for a young, vulnerable television star! There are so many people around, I'm sure it is only a matter of time until they work out where I live and start following me home. Desiree told me a horror story about some crazy fan who worked out where she lived. He wouldn't leave her alone. The more I think about Danny's suggestion, the more I think I should move to a safer area.

January 22

11.45p.m.   Jerry's Junk-yard

I thought I had tonight off. Think again. Tamara bundled David and I off to a movie premiere which turned out to be more like a photo session. There must have been a dozen photographers outside the cinema, but they weren't snapping the other celebrities – they were snapping David and I! Apparently a couple of the gossip columns here have picked up the Perth story and are convinced we are an item. David and I didn't say anything to confirm this, but the fact we arrived together and are doing such a convincing job of falling in love on screen seems to be all the evidence they need. On top of all this, David and I only had one cab charge so we had to share a taxi home. One photographer got a shot of us leaving together. Very incriminating! I must admit the whole adventure was fun, but what is Danny going to say when the pictures are published?

January 23

3.35p.m.   Channel Five

My worst fears have been confirmed. I've just had a call from Danny. He's seen the shots of David and I in the paper, running with the headline 'TV Couple Together'. Danny wants to see me later tonight, no doubt to give me a hard time about it. He's not the only one who is upset. I also found a note from Marianne, David's girlfriend, in my pigeon hole. It reads: 'David and I are very happy together. Don't get in our way.' I couldn't believe it. I have seen her hanging around the studios, keeping a close eye on the rapport between David and me (of which there is hardly any). She is *so* protective of him. Marianne's no beauty queen, and she hasn't got the most glamorous job, but *I'm* not about to make a move on her boyfriend. She seriously thinks I'm trying to steal him!

10.30p.m.   Jerry's Junk-yard

Cruising. Everything is fine with Danny. He fully understands the publicity machine, in fact, he encouraged me to play along with the real life romance. He thinks it will be very good for my career. But what do I think? Well, I agree it will generate lots of press and bolster my profile. I guess it is worth it.

January 24

11.45p.m.   *Jerry's Junk-yard*

I took a deep breath, laid my cards on the table and told Jerry and Kent exactly how I feel about our living situation. I told Jerry I am tired of coming home and finding a different girl in the kitchen. I don't care how many relationships he has, I'm just sick of him bringing them into our home. I also told Kent I have had enough of him rehearsing until all hours of the morning. And I've been noticing a few items from my make-up kit disappearing, most notably my shocking red lipstick. I know Kitty Kat has been using them as part of her act! They were both apologetic, promising to be more considerate in future.

Afterwards, Jerry suggested he take some shots for my portfolio. His way of showing just how sorry he is. I wasn't really in the mood for it, but I could tell he was genuine in wanting to make amends so I agreed. We went downstairs into the underground carpark. There was nobody coming in or out. I wore the wild card dress from the Miss Bondi Contest. Jerry loved the ripped look, and since the dress has probably done its dash, I allowed him to rip it even more for the effect he wanted. The photo shoot is more like a story, with me playing the part of a savage girl who lives in the

83

carpark. I have to admit we may have gone a little far with the dress. By the end of it, I was hanging out from all angles! But the shots were fun, and I will be the only person to see them.

January 25

8.30p.m.   Jerry's Junk-yard

Another weekend is over. I spent the day with Danny, who apologised for not being able to see me last night. I had been disappointed, but after last weekend and today I have no need to doubt his feelings for me. I persuaded Danny to take me to his parents' house. I wanted to see where he lives, get a glimpse into his life and what makes him tick. Well, a glimpse is all I got. We stopped outside. His family home is a mansion in Vaucluse, complete with swimming-pool and tennis court. Danny didn't want to go in. His mother and step-father were having a garden party, which I could barely see through the thick hedge. I got the feeling he doesn't want me to meet them, or vice versa. Am I not good enough? Would I embarrass him? Danny assured me I would meet them when the time is right. I stopped myself from questioning it any more, and allowed the day to pass and his company to fulfil me.

I'm now in bed, learning my lines. David and I have our first passionate kiss tomorrow. Crisis!

January 26

I have just washed my mouth out with soap. David not only kissed me, he forced his tongue down my throat and attacked my tonsils! I couldn't believe it – in front of the crew, the extras and the other cast! The director – Simon is back – thought it was the most convincing acting David has ever done. Unfortunately, that was no acting! David really enjoyed it. Worst thing is, today was only a rehearsal – tomorrow we have to do it all again. Just when I finally divert Casper's attentions (he's lusting after one of the extras), I now have to contend with David! I think I have a real problem on my hands.

January 27

8.45p.m.   *Jerry's Junk-yard*

I had a quiet word with David this morning, just before we went on set. I reminded him we were just acting and don't have to do a fully fledged kiss. I thought he got the message, but when the cameras were rolling, he did it all again. A full-on tongue sandwich! There were all these technical problems so we had to do it over and over, until finally, on the seventh take, we got it right. I felt like punching David, but there was a *Woman's World* journalist on set so I had to maintain I was enjoying every minute of it. This real life romance idea is hard work.

Later, the journalist interviewed us and David confirmed we were a couple. I just sat there, squirming, as though my life was flashing before me but there was nothing I could do.

I had a chat to Desiree about it. She is my only true friend on the show and, as an actress, understands my position. Desiree had a similar experience, only more personal. Tamara convinced her to do a story on the death of her parents. Desiree didn't really want to do it, but as she was just starting on the show, felt obliged. The story was completely unsympathetic. It graphically described how they died and depicted Desiree as angry and out for vengeance. For weeks Desiree couldn't go out without people asking her about it, dredging up painful memories. Although mine is a more superficial situation, I don't know how I am going to handle it. One thing is for sure. I have to convince David we are only acting.

January 28

8.45p.m.   Jerry's Junk-yard

I feel like death warmed up. Today has been non-stop. David and I are in practically every scene. The cast, the crew – everyone – is speculating about what is going on between us.

I popped into PMT on the way home and saw Danny. He wasn't all that happy that I had shown up unexpectedly. He hustled me out to a back room away from all the action.

I felt we needed to talk about the situation with David, but once again he was perfectly calm and collected about it all. He's happy to go along with whatever is best for my career.

I really need to sleep all this away . . . but what the hell is that noise? It's Kent and his Abba music again! So much for his promise to be more considerate. I've had enough of this.

January 29

4.45p.m.   Channel Five

I woke up this morning filled with new resolve. The sun was shining through the blinds, the birds were chirping. I showered and changed, feeling better about myself and my life. Everything was perfect until I stumbled over an old drunk who had decided to camp on our doorstep. This, combined with Jerry and Kent's antics, convinced me I had to move. I phoned Danny and asked for his help. This was partly an excuse to phone him, as I felt funny after last night and wanted to make sure everything was OK between us. Danny couldn't have been more supportive. He took time out of his busy schedule, picked me up from location and took me flat-hunting. We only had time to look at a couple of places before I had to report for studio. I think I've hit the jackpot with one of them. A great apartment in Double Bay, within my price range. I'm going to ring the estate agent and put in an application.

January 30

Great news. I have the apartment in Double Bay! I was having a lousy day at work, fumbling my lines and missing direction then, just when I was about to throw myself in front of the location van, a call from the estate agent came through. Danny is going to help me move. He's picking me up in a few minutes and taking me out for dinner. There's another launch at PMT afterwards, but I'm so tired I'm not sure if I'll be able to make it. In any case, I have about five minutes to break the news to Jerry and Kent. Wish me luck.

January 31

11.30p.m.   Melanie's penthouse

Home sweet home! I'm finally settled into my very own place – no flatmates, no noise, no drunks on the doorstep! The move wasn't hard. I have virtually no furniture, so the place is quite empty. The apartment is small but has two bedrooms, should I decide to get a flatmate. Not exactly a penthouse, but that's what I'll call it! I phoned Mum and Dad to tell them I've moved. Their reaction was mixed. Mum is pleased I am out of Kings Cross, but Dad still wants me to move home. Neither of them like the idea of me living alone. I assured them it is a building with security and I am safe and happy.

Jerry and Kent didn't take the news of my departure well, especially since I only agreed to pay them two weeks' rent. To escape the bad atmosphere, I decided to go to PMT last night after all. Everyone was staring at me, which made me feel very uncomfortable. Danny kept his distance, supposedly because he doesn't want to break the illusion of David and I being a couple. I know this is kind and understanding of him, but all I wanted to do was be by his side and share every moment with him. That's what I'm doing right now. Pity he's fast asleep.

February 1

8.30p.m.   Melanie's penthouse

A new month, a new apartment. Mum and Dad came over to give it the grand inspection, or should I say the thumbs down. The longer we are apart, the more distance there seems to be between us. This can only be a symptom of how much I am changing, how much my new career and outlook are affecting my personality. They made one last ditch effort to get me to move home. They told me how they have had to change their phone number. Entwhistle is such an unusual surname it hasn't taken long for fans of the show to find it in the directory and they have been ringing everyone in the family looking for me. A few guys even showed up at Auntie Roberta's. She had to call the police! All of this made me feel guilty, but I didn't buckle and agree to return. Now that I have found this great apartment, moving back is the last thing on my mind. At long last I think they finally accepted this.

The visit ended well, but the next couple of hours were sheer hell. I desperately wanted to see Danny, but I couldn't get hold of him anywhere. I've left messages, so hopefully he will call me soon. The guy is such a chameleon. He's always changing colours, always making himself impossible to find. I get the feeling he had an unhappy childhood and that this is his way of coping.

February 2

5.30p.m.   Channel Five

Newsflash: 'I'm In Love With Melanie – David Davidson Tells'. This is the headline from *Woman's World*, the magazine which was on set last week. The article reads like a Mills and Boon novel. The journalist – under Tamara's instruction – describes how we met at the audition and it was love at first sight. There are only a few quotes from David and I, inserted at critical points. The journalist also describes our first kiss and how we really went for it. David and I confronted Tamara who convinced us to maintain the act for a few more weeks. We are getting a lot of publicity – more than the rest of the cast – so it has its advantages. What's more, in a few weeks' time we can get extra publicity out of the break-up. The main thing that worries me is someone discovering the truth, that it is a ruse and we are making the whole thing up for publicity. We would both look like idiots and never work again!

February 3

7.45p.m.   Melanie's penthouse

I feel like a character in an Alfred Hitchcock movie. Here I am, sitting in my empty apartment, scared out of my wits. Somebody keeps phoning, then hanging up. I don't know who it could be. The only person I have given my new number to is the production secretary. There again, I suppose she handed it out to several departments so it could be anyone from work. Maybe I'm overreacting. Crisis: what was that noise? I can hear somebody in the stairwell . . .

10.30p.m.

False alarm. The footsteps belonged to Danny, my knight in shining armour. He's just made himself a bed in the spare room and is going to stay the night. I'm a little surprised he didn't want to crash with me. We have seen each other several times, often at night, but he has never made a move on me. I wouldn't mind if he did; however, the fact he is holding back is also appealing. He respects me.

February 4

We are on location in some national park and I just had the most embarrassing experience. I was busting to go to the toilet, but the portaloo is miles away, so I thought I'd quickly duck behind a bush and relieve the pain. Little did I know, there was a camera pointed in my direction and everything was broadcast over the monitor. The crew are in stitches! I am hiding in the wardrobe bus, waiting to do my final scene and trying to block out the laughter. I can hear David cackling the loudest. He's really getting on my nerves. This morning, as the runner was driving us out of the studio, there was a group of school kids at the gate. David purposefully put his arm round me. I know we are supposed to be going out together, but this is taking the joke too far. I think I'm in too deep.

February 5

8.30p.m.   *Melanie's penthouse*

I'm too scared to read tomorrow's newspaper, in case I'm in it: 'TV Star Murdered in Apartment'. I just received another series of crank calls, on the home phone and the mobile. I have called Danny and he is on his way over. Now I know this is not an isolated incident. Somebody is really after me! But who? Troy? Has he found out about Danny? Is it someone from the show, disgruntled about all the publicity I'm getting? I've just had another thought, straight out of an old *Mercy Hospital* storyline: maybe it is my parents, trying to scare me into moving back home? I can't believe I'm considering such things. I can hear Danny's car pulling up outside. Superman!

February 6

7.50p.m.   Channel Five

I think I know who my crank caller is. Marianne, David's girlfriend, is the exact type to resort to such scare tactics. I had another encounter with her today. She's furious that David and I are a public couple. Moreover, she has been on set often enough to learn my phone numbers. I'm sure Marianne has an evil streak. I thought about asking David to get her off my back, but I've come up with a better idea. I've bought a whistle, so the next time I get a call, I'll blow it so loud she'll never hear again!

February 7

7.30p.m.   Melanie's penthouse

Saturday. A day to catch up on sleep, wake up to the sound of music videos in the background and laze on the beach. Not a chance. David, Desiree and I were celebrity cooks at a sausage sizzle, I think it was to raise money for the homeless. The crowds went wild, pushing and shoving to get to the front of the queue. I turned so many pieces of meat it's made me a vegetarian! Not surprisingly, Marianne was lining up for her slice of pig. What did surprise me, or should I say unnerve me, was getting another crank call in the middle of it all. Marianne was standing right in front of me so it couldn't have been her.

I have told Desiree about the calls. She insists I change my numbers. If the calls persist, I'll have to notify the police. I'm trying not to get freaked out by it all, hoping it is just some silly kid. Danny has been very sympathetic. He even suggested he move in, if only for the time being. He's coming back later tonight and we're going to PMT (I know, yet again). I guess we'll talk about it then.

February 8

1.00a.m.   Melanie's penthouse

I'll have to start hiding this diary – Danny has moved in! I got a few more crank calls this morning so I asked him to come over. Next thing I know, he has his blow up mattress inflated in the spare room! I feel quite awkward. I am living with my boyfriend! I know it's only temporary, but this is a development in our relationship. Yet we haven't even slept together. When it came to time to go to sleep, we simply kissed then went our separate ways. I felt terrible allowing him to sleep on the mattress, while I have the comfort of my queen size bed. But I didn't want to invite him to share, just in case he got the wrong idea. Or is it the right idea? I always avoided sleeping with Troy, but

94

with Danny I feel different. I am so attracted to him, emotionally and sexually. I guess it's my high moral Mosman upbringing that is keeping me back. Every time I think about Danny I hear my mother and father lecturing me: 'No sex before marriage!' But does it really matter these days? If you really love someone, isn't sex just a logical progression? I guess that's the question: do I love Danny?

February 9

8.30p.m.   Melanie's penthouse

Another day, another dollar. I've just finished doing a photo shoot with David. Jerry took the shots. I felt a little uncomfortable with Jerry after moving out of his apartment so hastily, but he was cool about it. He and Kent have found another flatmate, some mild and meek secretary. Boy is she in for a few surprises!

On the home front, the crank calls have stopped. Danny isn't home – I guess he is still at PMT – but I still feel his protective presence. I had my numbers changed today, so that should throw the culprit.

I have a busy day tomorrow so I'd better learn my lines. Later.

February 10 & 11

7.30p.m.   Channel Five

I'm going to vomit. I've just come from the studio, where

the cast and crew are giving Norma a going away party. I've never seen such a display of false sentiment in my life! Yet they are all acting like her best friends who are never going to see Norma again! Well, I know exactly how Norma feels about me so I'm staying right out of there.

I am about to find out who are my true friends on the show. Danny suggested I throw a house-warming party to cheer myself up. Now my crank caller has been thrown off track, I need to get rid of the bad vibes in the penthouse and fill it with good ones. I have handed out invitations to the cast and crew. I wonder how many will show.

February 12

10.00p.m.   Melanie's penthouse

Danny and I have been talking. He's really happy living here and, if I'm happy with the arrangement, wants to move in permanently. Heavy stuff. Danny says he's tired of living at home and, even though the crank calls have stopped, I still need protection. True. I am worried about intruders. But I'm also worried about Danny. He may be happy to stay in the spare bedroom for now, but in a few weeks' time? I'm still not sure if I want to sleep with him. Funnily enough, our situation is being echoed in a *Mercy Hospital* scene I am doing with Angie tomorrow. Veronica, her character, asks Sasha whether she should sleep with her new boyfriend, Rocko. Veronica says, 'If I don't sleep with Rocko I'll lose him.' I guess this is also true of my situation with Danny. I don't want to run the risk of losing him either. Guess I'll have to wait until the next episode to see how Sasha responds.

February 13

What a day! I started location at six-thirty in the morning, then went to the studio, then back to another location. Now I'm back in the studio – still two scenes to go! The atmosphere on set is much better with Norma out of the picture. David and I have split up in the storyline, which means I get a break from his method-acting smooth scenes. Unfortunately, Sasha and Vince soon get back together, so I'm sure it will start again. Most of my scenes are with Angie. Veronica has become Sasha's best friend on the show. Angie is a real space cadet. Billy was the first to tell me about her cocaine habit. She delivers her lines in a zonked out, android-like tone. The lights are on but there is definitely nobody home! I find her really difficult to work with. She never wants to run the lines beforehand. Also, she always changes her performances from the way we did it in rehearsal. This is so frustrating.

I'm actually quite glad I have a late finish. Danny should be in bed (if he's not working) when I get home, so I won't have to give him an answer about moving in permanently. Crisis: I've just remembered my house-warming party. It's two nights away. I have a lot of organising to do!

February 14

If I had a couch I'd be crashing on it, but instead, I'm curled up in a bundle on the floor. Today has been exhausting. I found a note from Danny, inviting me to PMT. I'm too tired to go; I have a big day tomorrow organising the party, waiting for everyone to show up . . . no doubt taking all the decorations down when I am left on my own! I'm really worried about it. None of the cast or crew have said anything, except Desiree and David. They've both promised to come. I thought about inviting my Mosman friends, but I figured they would feel out of place. OK, *I* would feel out of place. I don't want to sound like an uppity snob, but they just wouldn't fit in. The Nadine and Troy situation is also difficult. I don't want to see either of them. Nadine has sent a few letters along the lines of 'Can we talk?' I have told Mum not to give her my new phone numbers. Nadine has been a life-long friend, but I can't deal with any of that now. In fact, at this very minute, I can't deal with anything at all. I need sleep!

February 15 & 16

8.45p.m.   Melanie's penthouse

My party last night was a hit. I'll start at the beginning. Danny supplied the lights and borrowed a DJ for the night.

Just when I thought he'd gone to all the trouble for nothing, the first guests started arriving . . . and didn't stop! Everyone from the show put in an appearance. It was wild! I was the centre of attention and enjoyed every minute of it. There were laughs (Desiree got completely drunk), tears (Marianne turned up and whisked David away) and even danger (Brad nearly fell off the balcony – showing off as usual). Jerry and Kent showed up – Kent in Kitty Kat garb.

I finally managed to get rid of everyone around two, leaving Danny and I. It was a fantastic night for the two of us. We've never been closer. But, for moral and emotional reasons, I'm not sure that I'm prepared for a serious commitment. I have so much going on in my life – the show, my family – do I really have the energy for a serious boyfriend?

February 17

3.45p.m.   *Botany Bay Hospital*

This must be the worst job in the world. Sitting around all day in stifling heat, waiting for technicians to get their cameras to function and working with middle-aged actors who can't string two words together. I'm at the *Mercy Hospital* location. There is a problem with the camera, so all the material we have shot has to be done again. My scenes are with David and some guest actress named Hilda. She's in a washing detergent ad, which sums up her range as an actress. So far I haven't come across one guest actor who has been any good, no doubt it's the reason they never get regular roles.

Danny crept in at three a.m. this morning. He crashed on his air mattress. I found a note saying he has a lot of work at his step-father's new club, Firecracker. He'll probably be home late again tonight, so if we miss each other we'll have to catch up tomorrow.

I spoke to Desiree about my dilemma. The fact that Danny went to his own room last night means he respects my privacy. However, Desiree reminded me that he is a man and only after one thing: sex. I already know I don't want the same from him. But I do like having him around, even though he's out most of the time! I have to make a decision.

February 18

10.45p.m.   *Melanie's penthouse*

I made Danny an offer. I told him I would like him to move in – into the spare bedroom. I couldn't look him in the eye as I explained the terms and conditions, for fear he would reject or belittle me. I told him that even though I like him I still hold a few traditional values and am not ready for that level of commitment. I want to take things slowly. A pregnant pause. I was sure Danny would scoff at the plan. To my surprise, he agreed! We both have busy lives, so more than anything, need a good night's sleep.

He's more than happy to stay in the spare bedroom. Whatever happens will happen – if we want it to happen. We didn't get the chance to talk any further, as Danny had to head out to Firecracker and I needed to learn my lines. This has worked out perfectly.

February 19

11.45p.m.   Melanie's penthouse

Nothing much to report. David and I got back together on screen, which meant another passionate kiss. Marianne was on set, so David played it soft. I guess she gave him a firm warning, probably after my party. Aside from this, Danny is at work. A few days ago I was worried about commitment, but the reality is I hardly see him at all. I'm not sure this is a good thing.

February 20

3.30p.m.   Channel Five

I have just read the funniest article. *Exclusive* magazine have done a story on famous real life couples. There are shots of Tom Cruise and Nicole Kidman, Goldie Hawn and Kurt Russell, Bruce Willis and Demi Moore – and David and me! Seriously, the publicity is getting out of hand. Three kids stopped and asked if it was true that we were going out together. I said it was. They looked so excited! I wish the other cast found it as amusing. They know David and I aren't together and resent the publicity we are getting. Apparently Brad and Angie were supposed to do the Perth telethon but Tamara bumped them in favour of us. She's even rearranged next week's schedules so we can do *Good Afternoon Australia*, a national talk show! Steve is calling my character. I have to go.

February 21 & 22

4.45p.m.   Hyde Park

I'm sorry I didn't get time to write last night. I finished studio really late and Danny whipped me off to Firecracker. This was my first insight into what Danny actually does, though it still remains a mystery. Danny seems to be his step-father's right-hand man, a trouble-shooter who walks round with a big gun in his pocket making sure everything is OK. I see him talking to his step-father on the phone, but aside from this, his step-father remains this shadow-like presence. Mr Big. Danny assured me I will get to meet him at the opening of the club.

Afterwards we went to PMT. I must admit I'm getting a bit tired of the scene, but Danny has to go there for work and it is so dark I can almost fade into obscurity. Almost. Every time I do get recognised, somebody always asks where David is. I tell them he has gone to the toilet. I can see them waiting for him to come back, but since he never shows, they must assume he has a bad case of indigestion!

I have slept most of the day. Danny is off at his parents. He didn't ask me to go along.

February 23 & 24

8.45p.m.   Melanie's penthouse

This week has been very relaxing for a change. Danny and I went out for dinner last night. Afterwards he went off to PMT, but I stayed at home.

I have a big week in studio coming up. We are filming a scene in which Sasha is told that a close friend who she grew up with has been killed in a car accident. The material is difficult and I don't know how to tap into it. Tamara has organised some meeting with a counsellor, for publicity purposes, of course. Hopefully this will give me an insight into how to play it.

February 25

7.35p.m.   Melanie's penthouse

I am trapped in a web of lies. David and I appeared on *Good Afternoon Australia* today. The interview was ostensibly about our characters, but the host, Don Chester, steered the conversation round to our personal lives. David and I didn't say much, but our silence gave the impression it was all true. The talk show was quite an experience. It was really nerve-wracking sitting in front of a studio audience. I remember my mum and grandmother going to tapings over the years – now I'm actually on it! It feels really weird. Talking of Mum, she saw the show on TV and called afterwards to find out what is really going on. I told her a few weeks ago that the story was all contrived, but this isn't what she wanted to hear. She thinks David is a lovely boy and that we should get together!

February 26

7.45p.m.   *Channel Five*

I hate Aldov! He is the most unsympathetic director in the world. Well, of those I have met so far. I've just finished doing the scene where Sasha reacts to the news of her friend's tragic death. I had to cry, which was really difficult. Aldov didn't appreciate this at all and kept on calling for retakes. By the end, I had taken so many eye drops my pupils were swelling. What's more, Tamara stuffed up with the counsellor so I didn't have time to talk to her before the scene. Flora helped me a little, suggesting I visualise a painful memory from my past and apply it to Sasha. I'm now crying for real. Aldov called me up to the control room and gave me a lecture about concentration. I was too scared to retort, but I truly think he is out of line. Desiree agreed with me. He gives her a hard time as well. You know, in all the times I worked at Pietro's Cafe I never felt as upset as this. Yet now, in my dream job, a few words from a cruel director make me feel like slitting my wrists. I know I've managed to hold my chin high before, but this time I can't. It's all getting too much.

February 27

Lots to say, no energy to say it. Danny was very supportive last night. He's moved a lot of his furniture over, including a couch, which we ended up falling asleep on. I was beginning to think that living together has taken the shine off our love life, but after last night, I know it hasn't. He knows exactly the right thing to say and how to say it. Having said this, his here-one-minute-gone-the-next behaviour is really getting to me. He's off at some club tonight, I'm not sure which one. I know he has his life and I have mine, but I want him to be here. I feel there is still a big question mark; a side of his life I still don't know about.

February 28

2.30p.m.   Channel Five

I have to hand it to Tamara – she really knows how to get a story. I did a photo session with the counsellor this morning, two days after the friend's tragic death scenes. I had to pretend I was researching the part, even though it is too late to apply it to my performance. This weekend is a big one. David and I have shopping centre appearances. Later.

March 1

I am a megastar. OK, a superstar. Our shopping centre appearance was amazing. People screaming our names, throwing presents on to the stage and trying to touch us. The suburb was way out west, the heart of viewerland. These kids have no life, no money. They fear for their future. The only thing that keeps them going is our characters, their heroes and heroines. I noticed a few of them styling their hair in pony-tails, which is how Sasha wears her hair on the show. They are all trying to be me! I never realised my work had such a profound effect on their lives. Security had to escort us to our cars – there were people everywhere trying to follow us or find out where we were going. I'm quite dazed by it all.

Danny is at PMT. He wants me to meet him there later on. I'll probably only make it for an hour.

There was a message from Mum on the answerphone, complaining that I never take the time to see them. I can hardly remember what they look like.

March 2

10.30p.m.   Melanie's penthouse

I've been putting it off for weeks, but with no more excuses left, I had to do it: I invited Mum, Dad and Sebastian over to dinner. I thought my plan would be foolproof; I'd say

Danny was my flatmate. He has a room of his own, where he stores all his possessions, giving the impression our relationship is strictly platonic. Or so I thought. The main course – eaten on our laps as we don't have a dining table – seemed to be going well. Mum talked about David Davidson, hoping to find some truth in the rumours. I soon put an end to the subject. Then Sebastian opened his big mouth and asked the obvious question: 'Are you and Danny dating?' I froze for three seconds, then recovered to give an Oscar-winning performance. I made up a huge story about how Danny is a devout Catholic and has strong attitudes about relationships. Mum was very pleased to hear this. They all left relatively happy, five minutes before Danny came home. You're a legend, Melanie!

March 3

7.45p.m.   *Channel Five*

Green room blues. I've still got to rehearse a couple more scenes. Danny phoned this afternoon and asked me to stop by Firecracker on my way home. The dance floor is now in place, just in time for the grand opening this weekend. All the cast have been invited. He's really excited about it. I wish I felt the same.

Today is one of those days that seem to drag on. Simon is hardly directing at all. He's just going through the motions, which filters through the cast. None of us have any energy at all.

March 4

Tough day. The only thing getting me through was the thought of a party after work, for *Teen Scene* magazine. Tamara said the party was to celebrate their fifth birthday, so I thought it would be a chance to let my hair down and meet some interesting people. Boy was I wrong. The minute I got there they handed me a cocktail dress and asked me to put it on. Next thing David and I were thrust into the paparazzi. Tamara kept taking drinks from our hands, warning us not to get intoxicated until the shots had been taken. I had to pose with all these models and pop stars. At the time I was excited by it all, but now I think about it, I didn't enjoy myself. The atmosphere was so false, so pretentious. Nobody wanted to know me, they just wanted to have their picture taken with me.

March 5

8.30p.m.   *Botany Bay Hospital*

The nights are starting to get cold. I've just realised that I've missed an entire summer working long hours during the week, publicity at the weekend. I have hardly had the chance to go to the beach at all. I'm now hanging around on location. There are problems with the lighting. On top of this, there is a huge crowd watching which makes it really hard to concentrate on work. I'm really tired. I just want to go home and sleep.

March 6

7.30p.m.   Melanie's penthouse

At last an early night! Danny and I were planning to have a quiet dinner, but he had to dash off to Firecracker a few minutes ago. The launch is tomorrow night. I think there are big problems. He is really stressed.

March 7 & 8 & 9

4.30p.m.   Bondi Beach

Once upon a time my life was so simple. I used to have hours to write in my diary, laze in the sun and fantasise about my future. Now my fantasy has come true and I have no time at all. The Firecracker launch was quite, umm, eye-opening. I finally met Danny's parents. C.D. Greenwood is nothing like I imagined. Quite debonair and personable. Danny's mother, Giselle, is a different story. She lives a very high life – I've never seen anyone put away so much champagne in such a short space of time! Danny introduced me to both of them, though they didn't have much time for me – or Danny for that matter. His step-father stayed long enough to make sure things got underway. Then he left Danny to call the shots.

The club was pumping so much that nobody noticed

Danny and I disappear to the back room. That's when Danny's true colours began to show. He produced a small bag of 'goodies'. I'm talking about white powder, I suppose it was cocaine. Danny asked me if I wanted to do a line. I knew what he meant – how could I forget my experience with Maxwell and Annabella – but I didn't want to get involved. Horrified, I found myself making an excuse about feeling off-colour. I was too embarrassed to admit I had never done drugs before and didn't want to try. I pretended to go to the toilet.

I don't know exactly what Danny did or how much he did of it, but the next time I saw him he was as high as a kite. I ended up going home soon after midnight, but he came home at seven in the morning, then spent the rest of the day in bed. I didn't say anything about it, nor did he.

Last night was the first night Firecracker was open to the public, so Danny had to be there for that. Again, he came home in the early hours of the morning and slept it off. I didn't want to disturb him which is why I am at the beach. Unfortunately, a bunch of kids have spotted me and I'm sure it's only a matter of time until they make their way over. Later.

March 10

5.30p.m.   Channel Five

And the winner is . . . It won't be me, but I don't care. I

have my invitation to the *Exclusive* Magazine Awards! I've sat at home watching the awards for years but now, just as I dreamed, I will be there! Some of the other *Mercy Hospital* cast will be sitting at home. Desiree hasn't been invited, nor have Belinda and Todd, two other members of the cast. The network wants to push the new faces, the reason why David and I have been elevated to the top of the guest list. Brad and Angie are both nominated as Favourite Actor and Actress, so they will be there. *Mercy Hospital* has won Favourite Serial for the past five years, but this year it faces stiff competition: *Barossa Towers* has picked up in the ratings. I really want to take Danny, but Tamara insists David and I arrive together. The awards are in Melbourne so I'm going to surprise Danny with a flight. He can at least go to the after show party. I wish I had been on air long enough for readers to vote me Favourite New Talent. Next year!

March 11

10.45p.m.   Melanie's penthouse

The world of television is ruthless! Belinda and Todd both snubbed me today, simply because I have been invited to the awards and they haven't. Brad is also in big trouble with the rest of the cast. His agent, Dennis Starling, has found out how much the others are charging for appearances and offering Brad at a slightly lower cost. This reminds me – Sue-Ellen wants to start charging for my appearances. The spots I do for Tamara are part of my contract, but there are lots of other things I could do for extra money.

I wish Danny would come home. I have his ticket for Melbourne. I can't wait to see his face when I give it to him.

March 12

5.00p.m.   Channel Five

Danny Greenwood! The name makes me want to scream! I went to all the trouble and expense of getting him a ticket to Melbourne, then he tells me he can't go! There is some big launch at PMT which his step-father insists he attend. I refuse to believe Danny can't take one night off. His step-father doesn't run his life.

March 13

4.30p.m.   Channel Five

One more day to go! David and I had fittings for the awards. Tamara wants us to look the perfect couple, co-ordinated to the very last stitch. I'm wearing this sequined number, the full Joan Collins thing! I'm worried it will look tacky, but Tamara wants us to stand out in the crowd. As for Danny, I have that situation under control. He will be going to the awards; all I need to do is make one tiny phone call . . .

Why is it whenever I do something nice it all gets thrown back in my face? I phoned C.D. Greenwood to beg him to let Danny off the hook tomorrow night. A caring, thoughtful, compassionate gesture on my behalf. C.D. was only too happy to give Danny the night off. In fact, C.D. never told Danny he had to be there in the first place. So I tell Danny the good news. He hit the roof! He charged me with interfering in his work, running his life . . . I was so upset I cried for an hour. Well, all's well that ends well – I think. After much screaming and shouting, Danny made a few calls (which he didn't want me to hear) and agreed to join me for the awards. Of course, he will only be able to go to the after show party. He'll have to watch the ceremony from the hotel room.

I wish none of this had happened – I so desperately want us to have a good time.

March 14

1.45p.m.   Channel Five

'I'm so excited, I just can't hide it, I'm about to lose control . . .' I can't believe I know the words to a Pointer Sisters song! But that's the way I feel. I have a couple more scenes then I'll be jetting off to the awards in Melbourne. Tamara gave David and I a pep talk this morning: 'Don't frown. Don't drink. Don't swear . . .' Her last instruction: 'Look like a loving couple.'

Danny phoned this morning. He told me he's looking forward to going. I'm so glad he's calmed down. The more I think about it, the more I'm convinced he had another reason for staying in Sydney tonight. I just don't know why he lied to me. Hell, Steve is calling for Sasha. Later.

March 15 & 16 & 17

7.00p.m.   Melanie's penthouse

I'm going to have to employ a secretary – once again, I have so much to tell you! David and I sat together on a plane to Melbourne, arrived together at the hotel and shared a limousine to the *Exclusive* Magazine Awards. There were hundreds of people outside the theatre. David and I signed autographs for about half an hour. Photographers were taking shots from every possible angle. I have never experienced such a sensation, yet underlying it all, a feeling of falseness.

We made it to the lobby, where we were greeted with champagne and the sight of every famous star in the galaxy. I felt like getting *my* autograph book out! Then Brad spilt his drink all over me, so I had to disappear to the toilets. You'll never believe who was in there – Michelle! My idol! She had just flown in from London and was getting ready to present one of the first awards. She was telling me about when she was on *Mercy Hospital*. She has come so far since then, yet she still has fond memories. I wanted to ask her a million questions, but she did all the talking

– asking me about the crew and my plans for the future. Before we knew it the awards were under way and I had to rush to the *Mercy Hospital* table. I was placed next to David. Brad and his latest girlfriend – some Swedish model named Ulrika – sat opposite us. The *Barossa Towers* table was right next to us. Andre Blewitt (who I had met way back at the Miss Bondi party) sat behind me. Every time I turned round he was looking at me. I couldn't help but think of my old school books which were plastered with his pictures – now he is flirting with me!

The awards kicked off with a song from Don Chester. Thereafter, the show seemed to fly. Nobody was themselves. Everyone was too busy looking for the camera, trying to show their best angle. The big shock came towards the end, when *Barossa Towers* pipped *Mercy Hospital* for Favourite Drama. Casper nearly fainted! Brad still won Favourite Actor, but Natasha Manson from *Barossa* won Favourite Actress over Angie.

The show finished and the room dispersed, with talk of the various after show parties. There was one private after show party I had to go to first – in Danny's hotel room. I felt bad he couldn't go to the ceremony, more so because I was on David's arm. Danny didn't care. He told me he loved me.

As I was slipping into a cocktail dress, Danny produced a line of cocaine. I felt embarrassed. I know I shouldn't have been. All through school we were assured it was OK to say no and I believe this is true. I reached for the bottle of champers, took a swig and pretended to be too drunk to join in. I watched as Danny rolled up a twenty dollar note and inhaled the coke through his nostril. Then we went downstairs and hitch-hiked to the major after awards party. There I was – a television star – sitting next to some burly truckie driving through the city streets. It was such a crazy and impulsive thing to do. Only Danny could have thought of it.

We arrived at the party and followed the procession into a warehouse. It was pumping. The music had a European feel to it. Danny led me on to the floor. I could feel a fireball going through my body, burning me up and making me want to explode. I was so attracted to Danny. We danced, skin to skin, as though we were one.

I don't think I did anything I shouldn't have, but then again, I probably wouldn't remember if I had. This weekend has been too much.

March 18

9.00p.m.   Melanie's penthouse

I knew I'd have to crash back to earth sooner or later. You could tell which of the cast went to the awards on Friday night. We all had that hungover look about us. I gave Desiree a programme from the awards, just so she wouldn't feel as though she missed out entirely. Then, after rehearsals, David and I confronted Tamara. We told her we could no longer carry on the real life couple ruse.

Besides, Danny and I were obviously together at the after show party. *Exclusive* magazine will certainly be reporting on that. Since Tamara got us together in the first place, we ordered her to break us up. She tried to talk us out of it, but this time we stood our ground. I'm now at the penthouse, Danny is here and . . . wait for it . . . cooking dinner!

March 19

7.30p.m.   Channel Five

I wish the roof would fall in, we'd all be trapped and I wouldn't have to do another scene until the rescue men managed to pull us out. I have fifteen scenes in total today, full of tears, anger and subtext. Aldov is directing and, once again, giving me a hard time. The one bright spark to my day is Danny. He's phoned three times, just to see how I am and to tell me he loves me. You know what . . . I think I really love him.

March 20

10.00p.m.   Melanie's penthouse

Today started off bad but, for a change, ended up good. The bad start was an argument with Aldov, who said my performance was getting worse. I did a scene with David – the worst actor in the world – but Aldov actually had the nerve to say I was the one letting it down. The scene was about baking a cake. Aldov said I lacked motivation, that the cake represented Sasha's feelings for Vince – so she should be afraid of it flopping! I decided I would agree with him for the rest of the day, then plead my case to Casper. This got me nowhere as Casper and Aldov are old friends. Resigned, I came home hoping to see Danny. All I found was a note: 'Working on an exciting surprise. See you later.' There were hearts and kisses all over it.

I felt so in love with Danny that I had to tell someone. Why not my parents? I thought they might take slight comfort in the fact our love for each other is genuine, even though they're suspicious of him. So I paid them a visit. To my surprise, they had too much on their plate to worry at all. Sebastian is in trouble at school. I feel bad about not being there to support them, but I have my own life. Right?

March 21

8.45p.m.   Channel Five

I am so angry. Aldov is making my life a misery! He humiliated me in front of everyone today. David, Angie and I were doing a scene around the operating table. The dialogue was full of tongue-twisters, medical terms which sound professional but nobody will understand. We did about six takes throughout which I delivered perfect dialogue. Aldov kept calling for retakes. Too much light, not enough blood, more extras in the background! Then, during the seventh take, I made a slight mistake. He exploded! I was so furious I nearly walked off the set. The extras were all standing around, jaws gaping. David calmed me down, pointing out that Aldov is not worth getting upset over. I guess he's right. I can't wait to go home.

10.50p.m.   Melanie's penthouse

I couldn't go to bed without telling you about the 'surprise' Danny has been working on. Danny's best friend, Lex, has just started working for Southern Cross Records as a talent scout, discovering new artists and promoting them. Danny hopes to feature a lot of new acts in night clubs; a good cross promotion for both parties. I'm excited for him.

March 22

6.30p.m.   Channel Five

Aldov is the devil in disguise. He humiliated me again, this time coming down to the studio floor and demonstrating – in front of everyone – his interpretation of how I should play the scene. I was so upset I felt like crying. Anyway, Danny phoned and told me about some big launch at Firecracker tonight. I'm supposed to make a publicity appearance at a bowling alley, but I'm just not in the mood. I'm going to go out and have a good time.

March 23

My head is about to explode. I have so much to tell you, but this time, I don't know if I want to begin. Danny and I went to Firecracker last night. I have no idea what was going on. All I remember is wanting to forget my troubles and have a good time, no matter what the cost. But everything kept getting in my way. People recognised me from *Mercy Hospital* and were horrible. Night club crowds are very different to shopping centres; being on a soap gives you zero credibility in a night club. If anything, it makes you a laughing stock. Danny had the answer – a line of cocaine. I told him I didn't want to do it and stupidly consoled myself with some vodka. While he sat there snorting I returned to the dance floor. This time, if anybody hassled me I gave as good as I got.

Later, we went to PMT. Danny did a couple more lines. I remember arguing with him. Next thing I am having a good time again. Then, before I knew it, I was back at the penthouse, it was seven-thirty in the morning and Tamara was on my doorstep. She dragged me off to do an appearance on *Saturday Hits*. I had to put on some headphones, listen to a record, then do a review. The studio was spinning. Somehow I managed to do the review, but as soon as we switched to a commercial break, I was in the toilets vomiting my guts out. Tamara followed. Very unimpressed.

March 24

I have slept most of today away. I don't know my lines for tomorrow. I don't know where Danny is. I don't know the meaning of life.

March 25

5.30p.m.   *Channel Five*

Casper hauled me into his office, sat me down in the chair and launched into a huge tirade about my 'unacceptable behaviour'. Tamara told him about my disposition on *Saturday Hits*. Big deal. So I had a big night and wasn't feeling well the next morning. I work a seventy-hour week, then I'm expected to look bright and sparkling on the weekend. Forget it! I'm human. Casper, however, didn't buy this. He warned me that nobody was indispensable, though I'm sure this is just a scare tactic. Besides, David and I are on the cover of *Exclusive* this week. Our 'break-up' is the hottest story in town. Nobody else from the show gets that kind of publicity.

March 26

8.30p.m.   *Melanie's penthouse*

Work, work, work . . . that's all I seem to do. I have

discovered caffeine tablets. Now I can't get through the day without them.

The show has dropped a couple of ratings points in Melbourne, the lowest in several years. Casper is worried.

March 27

The penthouse is a mess. The last couple of weeks have been hectic for Danny and I, so housework has taken a back priority. Danny is off looking at some dance band signed by Southern Cross Records. I don't like the idea of him spending so much time at the clubs. I'm talking about the drug scene. I don't want to sound moralistic about it – I'm no Florence Nightingale – but I do believe he's taking way too many drugs. He insists he only does it on special occasions but I'm sure there are more of these than he's letting on.

March 28

3.30p.m.   *Channel Five*

I got to work this morning and *Mercy Hospital* is in chaos. The ratings have dropped even further and the network has ordered a major upheaval. The time-slot is moving from seven week nights to six, which pits us up against the news. On top of this, Casper plans to redecorate the sets, revamp the music and spruce up the wardrobe in the hope of attracting more viewers. What he didn't say is the thing on everyone's minds. Who is going to lose their jobs?

March 29

8.00p.m.   Melanie's penthouse

Tense. Tense is the word to describe the atmosphere at work. There were lots of suits on set today. Executive, sponsors . . . anyone who was anyone. There was also a big meeting with the writers this morning. I'm sure it will end in bloodshed. I know I have nothing to worry about. The writers will definitely keep Sasha in the show. Brad was talking about jumping the sinking ship, which wouldn't be good for the ratings. Although he has a massive ego and I'd like to see the back of him, he is very popular. I don't think he will leave. He's been on the show too long. He's typecast. The most surprising thing is that Casper asked Desiree to stay. She has a really good storyline at the moment and her fan mail has increased. Desiree, however, laughed in his face. Casper has been terrible to her, telling her to lose weight and dress better in public.

I can hear Danny at the front door. We are going to Firecracker tonight. I really need a drink.

March 30 & 31

All good things must come to an end. I haven't thought once about the show, my parents or the housework for forty-eight hours. Now, on Sunday night, the reality of Monday morning is setting in. Stop the world I want to get off!

April 1

4.30p.m.   *Channel Five*

I walked into the studio this morning and had to do a double-take – the hospital is a different colour! As part of the new improved *Mercy Hospital*, half the sets have been redecorated – without any explanation whatsoever. What's more, the latest set of scripts contained a few shocks. Sasha and Vince are getting married! They get engaged, organise the church and go on their honeymoon all within a couple of days! I marched in to see the head writer only to find a new face. Half the story team have been fired and replaced. Some fruit cake is now in charge. I sat down to talk to her about Sasha, only to find she has no idea of Sasha's background whatsoever. And this woman is writing the show!

April 2

There must be a law against working nineteen hours in one day. I had location at five-thirty this morning, followed by a series of interviews and studio tonight. Tamara has gone into publicity overdrive. I had to talk to all these journalists from suburban newspapers, the kind of press the show wouldn't normally worry about. They all wanted to know if I was heartbroken following my split with David. I got so tired of talking about it I was tempted to say it was all a ruse, but Tamara intercepted.

Then, in make-up, Billy dropped another bombshell – I have to have my hair cut and coloured. According to the memo from Casper, a new actress is joining the show with a look and style in conflict with mine. I am furious. I don't want to have my hair cut!

April 3

4.00p.m.   *Channel Five*

Just when you think you're doing OK somebody has to come along and steal the limelight. Larissa, the new actress is gorgeous – if you go for the skinny, flat-chested look. She's from Scotland – and loaded! Apparently, her stay in Australia is the culmination of her world travels. And that makes her an *actress*?

April 4

I feel awful. I have been so preoccupied with work I completely forgot about one of the most important nights in Danny's career. Southern Cross Records are launching a new dance band called Cardiac Arrest, developed by Danny. The launch is at PMT this evening, but I'm supposed to be going on *Into The Night,* the new Channel Five talk show. I'm scheduled to appear for the whole show, beginning with an interview and then drawing a competition at the end. The whole ordeal will take at least a couple of hours. What can I do?

April 5

2.30p.m.   *Botany Bay Hospital*

At long last I have a few minutes to catch my breath. I'm sitting at location waiting for the weather to clear so we can do a scene. I can hear the crew talking about me. Casper hauled me into his office once again. I didn't show up for *Into The Night,* claiming I felt sick. I knew this wouldn't go down well, but I could have got away with it – had I not been photographed at the Cardiac Arrest launch. I had to do it; Danny would have been so disappointed if I had missed his big night. Anyway, it was worth it. Much later on, albeit under the influence, Danny made a very interesting suggestion. He thinks I should cut a record. I haven't had the chance to find out if he was really serious. I hope he was! I'll have to talk to him tonight, by which time I hope he'll have recovered.

April 6

Kylie did it. So did Jason, Danni and Craig. So why can't Melanie Entwhistle cut a record? Danny was deadly serious about the suggestion. Apparently Southern Cross Records believe I have strong marketing potential. Danny is convinced I will be a megastar. I must admit I am quite excited by the prospect, especially as Danny is involved. Danny is organising a contract, which I will have to show to Sue-Ellen for approval to go ahead. It will take a couple of days. I can't believe this is happening!

April 7

I'm hiding behind the location van. There are hundreds of Japanese tourists buzzing about, excited by the cameras and video-taping everything in sight. I'm doing this stupid storyline where Sasha is locked into the opera house and gets caught up in a murder mystery. Don't the writers know this show is set in a hospital?

April 8

I knew it was too good to be true. I finally had time to go and talk to Sue-Ellen about the new musical direction in my career. She told me not to get involved. Can you believe it! She told me cutting a record would be bad for my career, especially since just about every other soap star has done it and the majority has failed. She thinks I will be a laughing stock. I know Sue-Ellen is against the idea because Danny is involved. A few newspapers have painted him as a fairly bleak figure, coming between David and me. This, of course, isn't true but I have to go along with it. Danny isn't home yet. I'll have to tell him what Sue-Ellen said. I know he won't be happy. Neither am I. I really want to be a pop star!

April 9

I'm going to be a pop star. Danny told me to defy Sue-Ellen. This is an opportunity of a lifetime and if I don't take it, I may never get the chance again. He told me to give Sue-Ellen an ultimatum: either she supports me on this, or I get a new agent. I'm nervous about taking such drastic action, but this is something I really want to do and I know I can make it work. Besides, what kind of agent gets in the way of advancing their client's career?

April 10

4.45p.m.   *Channel Five*

I no longer have an agent. I talked to Sue-Ellen this morning. I got quite angry with her. So angry, in fact, I fired her as my agent! I know I talked about doing this, but that was just talk – I never actually planned to do it. Even worse, I'm having a terrible day at work. What is my world coming to?

April 11

5.30p.m.   *Channel Five*

I didn't need today. I didn't need some uppity bitch named Larissa coming on set, acting like she owns the show and showing me up in front of the director. We did a scene in the cafe where Sasha is supposed to start crying. I worked myself up to it, then Larissa came and asked a really stupid question. She destroyed my emotional line. Our new director hates me and we hardly even know each other. I also hate the way they cut my hair – another consequence of Larissa's arrival. The worst thing is, she is so nice to me on set. She's nice to everyone. They all love her – especially David. For once I feel sorry for Marianne.

April 12

10.45p.m.   Melanie's penthouse

It's really happening! Danny has just given me a fifteen page contract from Southern Cross Records. I can't understand any of the terms or conditions, but Danny says it's all standard procedure. My contract for the show looks similar. Legal jargon. I phoned my father and he said he would show it to our family lawyer. I trust Danny and I'm sure he wants what is best for me.

April 13

4.00p.m.   Channel Five

Going crazy. Studio running late. I met Danny for lunch. I'm really worried about not having an agent. Sue-Ellen will represent me on matters to do with *Mercy Hospital*, given she negotiated the deal in the first place and has the right to claim a percentage until my contract expires. It's a worry because I should be out there securing personal appearances, making money like the other cast members. Danny has the perfect solution: he has had plenty of experience booking people for his night clubs, so he could easily work on the other side – that is, get appearance deals for me. Many in his step-father's clubs. In the meantime, I'll look for another agent.

April 14

I'm never wearing that tight nurse's uniform again! I've just spotted a memo from Casper to the wardrobe department suggesting I wear a push-up bra in every scene to improve my 'non-existent bust'. I know I haven't got much, but I didn't think it was such a problem that the producer would have to issue a memo over it. Anyway, what about that stick-insect, Larissa?

April 15

10.00p.m.   Melanie's penthouse

There is only one answer. Breast implants. Billy was right – Juanita admitted to me she had the operation, and it has done wonders for her career. In fact, she auditioned for *Mercy Hospital* three times over the years. She finally got the part after the implants! I've made an appointment to see a plastic surgeon tomorrow. I know the process is painful and expensive, but it is an investment in my future . . . right?

April 16

4.30p.m.   Channel Five

I wouldn't have silicone implants to save my life! I saw a plastic surgeon, Dr Sheree Shore, who gave me all the gory details. Apart from the pain, the healing process takes weeks – there's no way I could work at the same time. I was, however, attracted to the idea of puffing up my lips. I'm thinking about making a booking for Christmas.

April 17

5.25p.m.   Channel Five

Danny has secured my first appearance as a guest DJ in a night club this weekend. He's paying me eight hundred dollars! We decided he would take ten per cent commission, which would then cover his share of the rent. Work wise, Larissa is really getting on my nerves. The more everyone else likes her, the more I hate her. She told *Exclusive* she is going out with David. I guess Marianne didn't stand a chance. Now it looks like David dumped me to go out with her!

April 18

6.00p.m.   Melanie's penthouse

Today I had to be friends with people I don't even know. I had to take a family of competition winners on a tour round the studio. They asked a thousand questions I didn't know how to answer. What does this do? Why is that there? Who, what, when? I felt like saying 'How the hell would I know?' and telling them to bother someone else, but I kept my cool. It wasn't their fault. They were really excited to be there. And to meet me!

April 19 & 20

3.30p.m.   Hyde Park

My weekend is almost over, yet this is the first chance I have had to sit down and collect my thoughts. I did the appearance at Hot Ticket, a club out in the suburbs. The crowd are much more down market, and that's why they all knew who I was and thought I was great. I went on stage. The crowd went mad. I said 'Hi, are you having a good time?' I was so nervous the microphone was shaking in my hand. I stood there and looked pretty for about twenty minutes before being escorted away by security guards. There were people trying to touch me and pull my hair. Someone managed to get my watch off. They're probably showing it to all their friends right now, making up some story about me being their best buddy and how I gave it to them. All in all, I had a good time. I still get a buzz from seeing how happy the crowds are.

So now it is Sunday. I don't want to go home because the penthouse is a mess. It's a huge week for me at work, so many lines to learn and I haven't even started. My life is getting more crazy by the minute!

April 21

I've just signed my life away. Well, I've signed the contract for Southern Cross Records. Dad's lawyer looked at it and said it was legitimate. There are lots of out clauses which basically give the company the right to terminate the deal if the record isn't satisfactory, though I will still be paid for my time and effort in the studio. Danny says this is a standard clause and besides, the record is going to be great. He talked to Lex, his friend who will be producing the record, about what the actual song will be. They think a cover version would be better to begin with, something sure fire which will establish me and work on the dance floor. I can't wait to get stuck in.

April 22

8.00p.m.   *Melanie's penthouse*

More drama at work. Jerry has been fired from the show. They simply felt his shots weren't up to scratch and will be putting on a new photographer. I feel really bad. I like Jerry and he has done a lot for me. He doesn't deserve to have this happen to him. Casper has the network on his back and most of the blame is being put on publicity. Tamara is working her butt off day and night, which will mean more work for us.

April 23

I feel special. I've just come back from the children's hospital and realise I am a worthwhile person. Tamara surprised me this morning with the news that I had to do another appearance. I thought it would be another shopping centre fiasco, but it was something much more special. I met Alan, a ten year old boy with leukemia. His one wish in life was to meet me – his favourite TV star. I went to his room. He was so small and frail, but his face lit up the moment he saw me. I wanted to burst into tears. Here I have been, complaining about trivial things like publicity, then I meet a kid who really has problems. I feel like going to a park, sitting under a tall tree and writing a list of all the things I have to be grateful for. I know there are many and if I could put them in perspective I'd be happier. But I've got too many lines to learn . . .

April 24

7.30p.m.   *Melanie's penthouse*

'I Know You Want Me'. Sound like a number one hit? Well, it better be. I wasn't sure when I first heard it, but Danny and Lex (the producer) can remix and make it sound more upbeat and Nineties. I've listened to it about four times and yes, I think it has potential. The problem starts when I sing it. Danny assures me I will be able to get into it when I practise with a backing tape, which Lex will give me when I meet him. We're going out for dinner tomorrow night.

April 25

11.00p.m.   *Melanie's penthouse*

Danny and I have just come home from dinner. Lex is great. He's twenty-five – at last a producer who isn't old enough to be my father! He and Danny have been friends for years. We all get along really well. Southern Cross Records have a strong marketing department and with Danny's night club connections, we seem to make a strong team. We can't get any recording time for a couple of weeks so until then I am going to practise my vocals. Lex gave me the backing tape so now I have no excuse.

April 26

8.30p.m.   *Channel Five*

Studio is running late. I'm not going to get home until eleven. I'm really tired.

April 27

7.45p.m.   *Melanie's penthouse*

I have been busy practising 'I Know You Want Me'. The revamped music is too fast – it is impossible to fit in all the words from the original. What's more, I sound terrible! Like chalk on a blackboard! I think I need to invest in some singing lessons. Fast!

April 28

8.00p.m.   Channel Five

Crisis. I stuffed up so many times today, forgetting my lines, missing my mark. I made a fool of myself in front of everyone, most of all Larissa. She has the entire cast and crew twisted round her little finger! They all think she is the biggest talent in the world. That spoilt rich bitch really has it all.

April 29

8.30p.m.   Melanie's penthouse

At last something is working out. Danny – acting as my representative – phoned Casper and talked to him about my recording venture. Though it is separate to the show and should not intrude on my commitments, Danny thought it would be a good idea to have his support. Casper has mixed feelings. He hasn't liked me since I rejected his advances, so is never particularly happy about anything I do. But he had to concede that the publicity would be good for the show. We have his blessing and he will do whatever he can to juggle my workload.

April 30

I feel cheap. I feel nasty. I have been exploited by Jerry – the man who I lived with, who I thought was my friend. Remember the shots he took in the carpark where we used to live? The shots I thought were for my own exclusive enjoyment? Well, *Flash* magazine has run a four page spread with me in all my glory – except for a caption which reads, 'CENSORED'. How could Jerry do this to me? He has a right to be upset after getting fired from the show, but he shouldn't exact his revenge through me! I don't know if Casper has seen the magazine, but I know I'll be in big trouble when he does. And what about my parents? And Danny? I want to hide from the world.

May 1

The phones haven't stopped ringing. Tamara is run off her feet taking calls from newspapers and magazines asking for my side of the story. Tamara thinks I should implement damage control, claim I was tricked into posing for the shots. Casper is furious. I can tell he's going to make my life very difficult, probably by refusing all liberties I need to fulfil my recording deal. But the person I'm most worried about doesn't even know yet – Danny. I'll have to tell him. What am I going to say?

May 2

Danny isn't even angry about the shots. He simply offered me a line of coke and told me to use it to my advantage. He suggested a more adult, sexier image would be good promotion for the record. I'll be the Donna Summer of the Nineties! I am furious. I refused to take the coke. I had to get out of there. I'm now at Desiree's. She appreciates how bad this is for my career and although she doesn't have a solution, has made me feel a lot better.

May 3

I've just closed the door on a journalist and photographer from *Woman's World*. Tamara organised the story, my chance to tell the truth behind Jerry's photos. I told the journo that I only intended the shots for personal use. I never thought they would be published. I said I was deeply upset about what had happened and had learned from the experience. The photographer kept snapping away, capturing every tear as it rolled down my cheek. I didn't have to act. I haven't stopped crying since this terrible ordeal began. My parents have been ringing up wanting to know what is going on. The cast and crew are all talking behind my back. I even found one of the photos pinned up in the props department, which I promptly ripped down

in disgust. As for Danny, he's keeping a low profile. I
don't really want to see him.

May 4

4.00p.m.   Melanie's penthouse

I have just been turned away from a shopping centre
appearance. The manager said I was 'incompatible with
the image of his complex'. He made it sound as though I
took my clothes off every week. I tried to tell him my side
of the story, but he wasn't interested. The nightmare keeps
getting worse.

   As for Jerry, I found out he left the country. I'm tempted
to do the same.

May 5

3.45p.m.   Channel Five

I've spoken to Mum. I didn't want to return her calls
because I thought she would give me a hard time but, to
my surprise, she was sympathetic. She said she didn't know
what was going on but she knew I was in trouble and they
were there to help me. They told me to come over as
soon as I have the time so we can talk about it. I feel like
I have finally made a breakthrough. After all this time, all
the fighting and disagreements, thay are behind me. I'm
going to see them tonight.

May 6

It was so good to see my parents yesterday. I want to devote more time to them, but work is all-consuming. If only I lived closer to them . . .

Danny sure knows what buttons to press. I haven't seen him since we argued, but he has made it up to me. Dinner, flowers, chocolates . . . and a smiling face. He said he was sorry for upsetting me the other night. He only said the shots would be good for my image because he thought it would make me feel better. He also said he was proud of the way I handled the situation. On top of this, he offered to hunt Jerry down and have a go at him. I told him not to. I want to put this whole mess behind me.

May 7

I've just heard the worst recording of my life. It was me singing 'I Know You Want Me', captured on my portable tape-recorder. I was completely off key and couldn't keep up with the backing track. The recording session is just a few days away. Crisis!

May 8

I've found the solution. I got my taxi driver to stop by a New Age bookshop on the way home. Angie told me about a book to do with the power of the mind, which teaches you how to overcome phobias and achieve the seemingly impossible. I've read the first chapter which basically says you simply have to believe in yourself. It also suggests you make up a chant which you must recite. Mine goes like this: 'I can sing high and low and in any key, I know I can do it – nothing can stop me.' I think it's working.

May 9

3.00p.m.   *Channel Five*

Yesterday I was the scarlet woman, today I am Mother Teresa. The *Woman's World* story came out, portraying me as a helpless victim – the first bit of publicity that has been actually true. I made the cover!

May 10

3.45p.m.   *Channel Five*

Shock horror! Sasha and Vince are getting married in three weeks' time! The latest batch of scripts are ridiculous. The wedding is interrupted by an earthquake! They end up getting married in an ambulance. Tamara is planning some competition where viewers can win the wedding dress and be an extra during the actual taping. Though it sounds like a lot of work, I'm sure it will be fun. I've always wanted to wear a wedding dress.

May 11

7.30p.m.   Melanie's penthouse

I have so much to do over the next few days. The recording session is less than a week away, but I'm keeping a positive attitude. I'm chanting and practising to the backing tape. I actually think I'm improving. I'll have a five octave range by my first international concert tour!

Danny is working, though I'm not sure where. Our relationship is going through a funny stage. We seem to see each other all the time for a couple of weeks, then hardly at all. We'll see each other this weekend as he's organised an appearance at some club in the suburbs. I can hardly wait. Not!

May 12

3.30p.m.   Melanie's penthouse

I have a couple of hours off. I know I should be learning my lines or practising the song, but I decided to go shopping instead. The book said I should wear something positive when I attempt the hurdle I am trying to cross, so I felt a new outfit was required for the recording session. Well, I couldn't decide so I bought five. I don't think I've ever spent so much money in one day. I also bought Danny a ring. I'm going to give it to him tonight. I'm cooking!

May 13 & 14

3.30p.m.   Melanie's penthouse

I'm getting really sick and tired of appearances. To make matters worse this one was in a disco and the crowd was young. Their attention was fully devoted to me.

It's now Sunday afternoon. I have another big week. Probably the biggest so far. We are shooting the scene where Vince gives Sasha mouth-to-mouth resuscitation and proposes to her! This is the first time I've looked forward to kissing David. Larissa is also in the scene so I'm going to make sure it takes at least ten takes to get it right. She'll be so jealous. By the way, Danny loved his ring. He promised he would never take it off.

May 15

7.30p.m.   Melanie's penthouse

I don't have time to write. Tomorrow night is the long-awaited recording session. I need to get all the sleep I can – it will be a late one. I'll be fine, provided I keep chanting: 'I can sing high and low . . .'

May 16 & 17

Last night was the night. I showed Danny, Lex, the sound engineer, the tea lady – anyone with an ear – that I couldn't sing. I was standing in this little studio with a huge sheet of glass to separate me from them. I was all alone, except for a microphone and the sound of my hollow voice. Lex wasn't impressed. Danny had led Lex to believe that I had a good range, but even I'm not that good an actress. I sounded like a walrus. Lex wanted to book extra time in the studio, but I had to speak up and say I couldn't go on. I told them I was getting picked up and driven to the studio at seven and still had lines to learn. Lex agreed to call it a night. He simply said I did just fine and that he would see me again the night after tomorrow.

May 18

7.00p.m.   *Melanie's penthouse*

I have given new meaning to the term method acting. I was doing a scene where Vince comes in and finds Sasha asleep in the staffroom. She should be working so he gently wakes her up. The first half of the scene went well, until the point where I was supposed to wake up – only I was really asleep. He started shaking me but I still didn't wake up. Steve called cut and they finally managed to rouse me. Everybody thought it was funny at the time, but when the word got back to Casper he wasn't impressed. Sleeping on the job is not a good move, especially when the producer knows it's because you're staying up late to make a record. We're recording again tonight. I hope I get through it.

May 19 & 20

4.45p.m.   Channel Five

My singing career is over – before it has even started. Last night was my second – and probably final – stint in the recording studio. Danny said 'I have faith in you honey, you can do it!' But the problems started the minute I walked in. There was a technical hitch which put us back a couple of hours. The studio costs a fortune to hire and Lex, as you can imagine, was fuming. The technical problem was finally resolved and I had to go back in.

To make things worse, some Grace Jones look-alike was hanging about the studio, batting her eyelids at Danny and Lex. She's some dancer called Marcia Love, and she is obviously hoping the boys will be her stepping-stone to stardom.

By midnight everyone was ready to call it a wrap. And throttle me. I asked Danny if he was angry with me, reminding him that he was the one who assured me I would be OK in the first place. He barked, 'No!' I knew this meant he was angry. Then Lex asked him to stay behind. When I left, they were in the midst of a very tense meeting.

Danny didn't come home at all last night and he hasn't been home all day.

May 21

3.45p.m.   Channel Five

I'm never going to get married. I've spent hours getting fitted for Sasha's wedding dress – long veils, short veils, high cut, low cut. I found our new wardrobe mistress irritating as hell. She wanted to see me in every shape and style, probably because she is terrified of losing her job like every other wardrobe lady before her. Our new photographer was there to photograph me in all the different designs. I'm so over it. I'm also over Danny. He hasn't phoned. It's now been two days and I still have no idea where he is. I have rung all the clubs, but they have no idea where he is either. This is not my idea of a relationship.

May 22

6.45p.m   Melanie's penthouse

Everything is back to normal. OK, OK . . . I know you think I'm weak and spineless. I know I said I was going to kill Danny. I would have except Lex almost killed him after our last recording session. Lex holds Danny responsible for the failure of the recording session. Danny had so much faith and confidence in me he had led Lex to believe I would be the next sensation when, in reality, I can't sing a note. The session was a complete waste of time and money. Danny, however, still has faith. He told me he's spent the last few days in a friend's private recording studio salvaging my vocals. He took the rough mix to Lex who agreed there was hope for my singing career. There was I storming about the apartment when all this time Danny was working day and night to help me. I told him he should have at least called and told me what he was doing. Danny said he didn't want to get my hopes up. He wasn't sure if he could do anything with my vocals. But now he's convinced there is something that can be used. Though I am pleased he went to this effort, another side of me wishes I could put the record behind me. I'm looking forward to releasing it, making a video . . . but what happens when someone wants me to sing live? I know lots of artists get away without singing on their records, but I'm not sure I can? Am I about to make a gigantic fool of myself?

May 23

7.30p.m.   Melanie's penthouse

I can't bring myself to do another appearance. Danny has booked me to appear at Flashlight, the club I used to go to when I lived in Mosman. I can just imagine what will happen. I'll get up on stage and see all my old friends. I haven't seen any of them for months but I know they talk about me, saying that I have outgrown them and that I am self-obsessed. I can't possibly subject myself to the humiliation. I'm sure Danny will understand.

May 24

6.00p.m.   Melanie's penthouse

Danny refused to take no for an answer. He convinced me to do the Flashlight appearance, assuring me it wouldn't be as bad as I thought. He was right – it was worse. Most of my old gang were in the audience – including Nadine and Troy! I felt really embarrassed. I saw them come back stage to talk to me, so I snuck out the back door and hopped into a waiting taxi. I made Danny find his own way home. I've hardly seen him at all today. He's been working on 'I Know You Want Me'. According to Danny, my voice sounds terrific. Southern Cross Records have planned a special pre-release party, which will be the first time any of us hear it. I think I should invest in some earplugs.

May 25

7.00p.m.   Channel Five

I am in such a good mood I thought it was about time I gave myself a treat. I've bought a new, red, convertible sports car! It looks gorgeous, even more so when I'm sitting behind the wheel. I've worked hard for this and

I'm going to get a lot of use out of it. The show is only providing transport for the first six months, so when they pick up my option I'm going to have to get myself to and from work.

I can't believe I've almost been on the show for six months. How time has flown!

May 26

11.30p.m.   Melanie's penthouse

'I Know You Want Me' is going to be a big hit. There's only one problem – I'm not the one singing it. Danny said he pressed a few buttons, added a few instruments . . . but I don't believe it. Nothing could turn my warble into the soft, silky groove that melted off the turntable. I've just come home from the Southern Cross pre-release party. The Southern Cross executives and marketing people were thrilled with the results. They said I am going to be a superstar. I smiled and went along with it, but I knew something was amiss. Finally, I cornered Danny and dragged him on to the balcony. I demanded to know who the vocals belonged to. Danny tried to make excuses, but then the voice herself appeared on the scene. Like Grace Jones, Marcia has a voice too! She looked such a tart and had the cheek to make some comment about our voices sounding great together. Danny squirmed uncomfortably, unable to deny Marcia's claims. I was furious. I had to get out of there – I demanded he drive me home. Danny said he couldn't leave. Marcia suggested I leave without him – she'd be happy to give him a lift back later. Danny didn't argue. He gave me his keys. I felt like shoving them down Marcia's throat, but I kept my cool and made a discreet exit. Danny and I are going to have a serious talk when he gets home.

May 27

4.30p.m.   Channel Five

I woke up this morning determined to focus my efforts on the show. I've allowed the record to use up my energy and I need to lift my peformance. The wedding is coming up in a couple of weeks and Sasha is in almost every scene, so I have to be on the ball. This attitude soon came unstuck. *Exclusive* magazine ran a story about the record, with quotes from Danny and Lex about how it is going to be a huge hit. I have tried not to say too much to the cast and crew, but now they have all read about it they are full of questions and can't wait to hear it. The more people talk, the more pressure I feel. I can't handle living a lie.

May 28

7.45p.m.   Melanie's penthouse

Talk time. I told Danny how I feel about the record. I can't go through with it. Danny assured me, as he always does, I have nothing to worry about. Lex wants to insert a rapper halfway through the song, so this will take a lot of the emphasis off the vocals. The final result will be a diverse mix of sounds. He pointed out that lots of famous pop stars rely heavily on back-up vocalists, especially those starting out. Then, as they perform and their voices grow mature, they come into their own. This made some kind of sense. In the end, I couldn't be bothered thinking about it any more. I'll just go with the flow . . .

May 29

11.30a.m.   Channel Five

I'm not sure what to make of the stack of green paper in front of me. I've just received amendments to next week's scripts, the week where Sasha and Vince finally get married. The storyline has changed. Vince jilts her at the altar! I thought this was probably the writers' way of drawing it out and the wedding would actually happen a couple of days later, but they seem to be going in an entirely different direction. Vince and Ebony, Larissa's character, appear to be getting together. What does this mean for me?

May 30

6.30p.m.   Melanie's penthouse

I feel like buying a gun and sticking it to Larissa's head. She is making my life a misery. We had to do four scenes together where Sasha tells Ebony she thinks Vince is having an affair. Larissa kept on changing her performance from the way we did it at rehearsal, which threw me completely. Aldov, the director from hell, called an early lunch and suggested I take the time to learn my lines. Although I knew exactly what I was doing, I decided to brush up just so they couldn't give me a hard time in the afternoon. I found a quiet table in the canteen, but as soon as I started to go through the scenes Larissa deliberately dragged David to the table right behind me. Larissa complained about the endless publicity she and David are going to have to do now that they are the next big couple on the show. She all but said Sasha was on her way out. I don't know how David puts up with her.

May 31

5.30p.m.   Channel Five

I'm putting out a contract on Larissa. There were lots of amendments so I made a point of learning them. Confident, I walked out on set and did a quiet read through with Larissa. We seemed to have it perfected, only when Aldov began the scene it became clear I had the wrong dialogue – someone had swapped the amendments in my pigeon hole. That someone must have been Larissa. She must have known I had the wrong scene when we did the quiet read but didn't say anything – she was obviously setting me up for a fall. Aldov came down to the floor and had a go at me. Larissa just stood there, smirking. I knew it was pointless to argue, so, tight-lipped, I marched off set and straight up to Casper's office. I told Casper that Larissa was sabotaging my performance. I could no longer do scenes with her. What's more, I wasn't going back to the studio. Casper pointed out how much time and money I was wasting, but I didn't care. I demanded he hear my point or I wasn't going back to set. Casper agreed to look into it on condition I return to the set. He'd better do something. I can't work with that bitch!

June 1

7.00p.m.   *Melanie's penthouse*

Casper had a talk to Larissa. He told her he was aware of a problem between us and advised her not to upset me! That was the only good thing to happen today – the rest of it has been a nightmare.

June 2

11.00p.m.   *The Doctor Juice Bar*

I'm sitting in a bar, on my third glass of red. Danny told me he had a long night ahead of him recording with the rapper, so I thought I'd pop down to the studio and cheer him up. I'm not sure who got the bigger surprise – Danny or me. There was no rapper, no Lex, no musicians – just Danny and Marcia. Danny had lied to me! I went up to him and asked him what was going on. He was completely off his dial. I could tell he was doing cocaine. I could also tell they were doing more than recording. Marcia looked equally trashed. Danny claimed the rapper couldn't make it, so he decided to take advantage of the studio time to polish a few additional lyrics he had written for the song. I didn't know what to say or think, so I walked out. I took a wrong turn and got lost in some back corridor. As I was trying to find my way out, I heard Marcia's voice echo through the silence. The lyrics were hot and sexy: 'Baby, baby, I want to be your lover, to me there is no other . . .' Danny kept on stopping her, telling her to put more emotion into it. He was getting off on it. I burst into tears and left. Now, sitting here on my own, I'm asking myself one question: 'Is he cheating on me?'

June 3

10.00p.m.   Melanie's penthouse

I've got a big day tomorrow. We're shooting the wedding, and once again there are thousands of changes to the script which I must learn.

I haven't seen Danny since last night. I heard him come home at seven this morning. I was awake. I hardly slept all night.

June 4

I'm in my wedding dress, propped up with strong gaffer tape and feeling anything but a blushing bride. We have about ten scenes to get through, beginning with happiness and ending in despair. This is a very emotional day for Sasha. Tamara is running round like the mother of the bride, instructing our new photographer to take shots of everything from the bridal party to hundreds of fans who have lined up outside the church to watch. Apparently some radio station broadcast where we were shooting. Tamara blames it on an inside leak, but I'm sure she let the announcer know in a bid for much needed publicity.

Unfortunately, I have to do several scenes with Larissa as one of the last minute changes was to make Ebony a bridesmaid. David and Larissa are fighting, something to do with comments she made to a magazine about their private life. He tried to talk to me about it, but I have so many problems of my own I couldn't bear to take on his as well.

I really need to ask Danny about Marcia, but I'm worried the answer may not be what I want to hear. Even if it is, how will I know if he's telling the truth?

June 5

I'm about to go to bed. The last two days have been exhausting, physically and emotionally. Danny still isn't home. He left a note to say dinner was in the oven and a surprise on the coffee table. The surprise is a story board for the video clip, which he and Lex want to shoot this weekend. This is like the first draft of a novel – the sketches of what is going to happen in each scene.

My life is crazy! I'm working eighteen hours a day on a show where everybody is at each other's throats; I haven't seen my family for a few weeks; I'm about to make a video for a song I didn't sing; and the only communication I have with my boyfriend is a note pinned to the refrigerator!

June 6

10.30p.m.   *The Gap*

I'm sitting in my car overlooking The Gap, the treacherous cliff where thousands of people have committed suicide. I'm tempted to do the same.

I had to escape the penthouse. It's all getting on top of me. I asked Danny about what happened with Marcia. He played it all down, assuring me they were doing just as he said – putting final touches to the song. I didn't have the chance to say anything more about it as he changed the

157

subject to the video clip. Somehow he has managed to wangle creative control over it.

I don't know how it's happened, but Danny has taken complete control over my life. When I first met him, he worked in a night club, now he is acting as my agent, securing me recording deals, which he seems to be in charge of every step of the way. Problem is, I don't have the time or energy to get on top of it. The more I think about it, the worse I feel. It seems so much easier to let him take the wheel, even though I fear we're on a collision course.

June 7 & 8

8.30p.m.   *Melanie's penthouse*

I woke up this morning determined to get my life in order. I can't continue to allow Danny to organise all my affairs, as well as share my apartment and have a relationship with him. So, I talked to a few of the cast at work and decided to get a new agent. I asked for their honest opinions of their agents and have a fairly good idea of who I should approach and who I shouldn't. I have a couple of interviews tomorrow.

June 9

3.30p.m.   *Channel Five*

I have a new agent. This is good news for me, but bad

news for Danny. I am now represented by Dennis Starling, who looks after Brad and Angie. He is one of the most respected agents in town and, according to Brad and Angie, very good at negotiating lucrative deals. For this reason, Dennis insists upon handling all aspects of my career. This includes acting, singing and personal appearances. I told him I have a one year contract with *Mercy Hospital* and that Sue-Ellen has the legal right to a percentage of that. As for the singing and appearances, Danny has been negotiating with Southern Cross Records and securing my appearances in his step-father's night clubs. Not any longer, says Dennis. While he can't do anything about *Mercy Hospital*, Dennis wants full control of my other interests. He also wants to structure a three year plan. Acting, singing and finances. I walked out feeling confident and reassured, but then remembered the bombshell I still have to drop – I have to tell Danny he can't represent me any more.

June 10

10.00p.m.   Melanie's penthouse

I'm sitting on the floor, amidst a pile of broken crockery. I didn't realise Danny had such a bad temper. I know he has every right to be angry. He has done so much for me – the recording deal, the personal appearances – and I am grateful. However, I have to do what is best for my career and this means going with a legitimate, reputable agent. I tried to make him understand that this can only be beneficial to both of us. Although I believe Danny negotiated a good deal with Southern Cross Records, an agent with the skill and expertise of Dennis will be able to do even better. He knows how much money the other stars are commanding and can negotiate better fees. Besides, Danny representing me was always going to be a temporary arrangement. Danny didn't see it this way, which made me start to think he only cares about one thing – having complete control over my life. I'm not going to let him do this any more.

June 11

4.30p.m.   *Channel Five*

Things have calmed down. Danny apologised for losing his temper last night. He assured me his main priority is my happiness and he won't get in the way. Just when I began to feel some sense of freedom, Danny started talking about the video clip which we will be shooting this weekend. He has a lot of grand ideas, most of which I am unsure about. I must be careful about the image I am going to portray, but Danny seems to have that worked out. I wanted to speak up and voice my reservations, but I didn't want to upset him. He has been understanding about my decision to join Dennis, so I better not rock the boat as far as this is concerned. The clip is to be directed by some guy named Wire, who has directed a lot of other well-known artists. Danny thinks his work is great, so I suppose that is one good thing. I'm not going to worry about it.

June 12

7.30p.m.   Melanie's penthouse

I'm sitting here on our very expensive leather lounge suite. Danny and I spent this afternoon on Oxford Street, trying to find something to wear for the clip. I was so exhausted going from boutique to boutique that I made him stop by a furniture store, simply so I could sit down and have a rest. Somehow, we managed to leave with a lounge suite – on *my* credit card! Danny said it would look great in our living-room – which it does – but my bank balance is less comfortable. He also talked me into buying several outfits for the clip, just so we have a choice on the day. I thought Southern Cross would pay for the wardrobe, but Danny wants to save the budget for special effects. Besides, he insists it's all tax deductible. We're shooting part of the clip at Firecracker. I hope it works out.

June 13 & 14

10.00p.m.   Firecracker

Sunday night. I should be snuggled up in bed, getting all the rest I need for another hectic week at work. Instead, I'm sitting in a smoky, dimly lit night club shooting an equally dodgy video clip. Danny and Wire keep changing their minds about the format. Their basic concept was to focus on different guys in night clubs who fantasise about seeing me on the dance floor singing 'I Know You Want Me'. There is a team of female dancers which includes – surprise, surpise – Marcia. There are smoke machines, blinding lights and special effects coming from every direction. The Firecracker sign is illuminated in the background, which I rise above on a platform supported by a makeshift crane. I'm supposed to look sexy but I can't see, breathe or balance myself for fear of the stage collapsing under me.

They have only one more shot to do. I'm supposed to rise off the stage and disappear through the roof, with the help of some invisible harness which will be attached around my waist. I've got a feeling I won't live to tell the story.

June 15

8.30p.m.   Melanie's penthouse

'One more incident like this and you're out.' The words of Casper Donald, our beloved producer, when I arrived two hours late for work. We were shooting the video until four this morning. I was so tired I slept right through my alarm. I was supposed to get up at seven and learn my lines, but I slept in and only woke up to the sound of my taxi outside. I was still half asleep when I got to the studio and in so much agony from wearing the harness I could hardly walk. The first scene was a major emergency and Sasha is supposed to bolt down the hospital corridor. I had all this complicated medical jargon on the way, which I kept on forgetting. Well, I didn't forget it because I didn't know it in the first place. Casper knew I was shooting the video over the weekend and reminded me the show must be my first priority. I wish Danny were here.

June 16

5.00p.m.   Channel Five

Rumour of the week: Casper wants to fire me. I saw a copy of a memo which Casper has issued to several departments. He wants my behaviour monitored and any problems reported back to him. I phoned Danny and told him what is going on. Danny reminded me I am still the biggest star of the show. He's right. I have the cover of *Exclusive* magazine again this week and *Woman's World* will be running the wedding story, so David and I will no doubt have another cover.

Danny has seen the rushes from the video clip and, despite my reservations, believes it is coming together well.

June 17

I'm sitting at home, all alone. Danny and Wire are off editing the video clip. I went and saw Dennis today. He talked about my three year plan. I told him I didn't think I would survive my year on *Mercy Hospital*. The atmosphere is very difficult. I also told him about my problems with Casper. He doesn't like me and takes every opportunity to criticise my performance and remind me I am at his beck and call. Dennis knows all about Casper's wicked ways. He told me about an incident a couple of years ago, when he was representing another actress on the show. Casper made a pass at her, but she turned him down. As a result, Casper fired her from the show. I told Dennis I think Casper feels the same way about me, and that he made a pass at me not long after I joined the show. Dennis was very interested to learn this. A little too interested come to think of it. I get the feeling he has something in mind.

June 18

Another long day. I had to squeeze into the wedding dress again for the studio scenes. We still have a couple more to go. Later.

June 19

I've completely forgotten it's Danny's birthday this weekend. His twenty-first! I can't let it pass without some kind of celebration – but there is so little time to organise it. Workwise, today was much the same as every other day. I don't know how I got myself into this situation. Tomorrow isn't going to be much better. Larissa and I are doing a fashion shoot for *Woman's World*. I also have scenes with her in the afternoon. No matter what bitchy comment she makes, no matter what she does . . . I'm going to be nice to her.

June 20

I tried and failed. We did a photo shoot at the Botanical Gardens, wearing the new spring collection while mounted on a horse. I have never ridden a horse before, but Larissa is an expert – well, with all that money she would be! I asked her how to mount, but rather than give me the correct instructions she set me up to get thrown from the horse. I fell right into a thorny rose bush, butchering the flowing white dress and leaving me with scratches all over. Afterwards, Larissa told the entire crew what had happened. They kept on making horse noises, throwing my concentration and making me forget my lines.

I'm at home now going through Danny's Filofax. I've decided what to do for his birthday tomorrow night: I'm inviting all his friends to a party at the Greenwich Hotel – one of the best in Sydney – as I don't have time to do anything here in the apartment. I have hired a room and caterers. I hardly know any of the people he has listed . . . except this one. Marcia Love. *She's* not invited!

June 21 & 22

6.00p.m.   *Greenwich Hotel*

I'm in tears. I'm sitting in the hotel room, or should I say what is left of it. The carpet is stained with wine and cocktails, ornaments smashed on the floor and every picture stripped from the wall. I'm too scared to look out of the window where one of Danny's stupid, immature friends decided to test the cliché – he threw the television set on to the pavement! According to the hotel, the damage bill is three thousand dollars! I have no grounds to argue. I left my credit card at reception to pay for the room, on top of which the hotel has promptly added the damage. As for Danny, he was coked to his eyeballs and didn't know what was going on. He and his friends – including Marcia, the slut – left at about three, following a promise of drugs in a seedy bar somewhere out in the suburbs. I was furious. I thought we would spend the night together, wake up this morning and reminisce about what a fantastic party it was. Instead, I woke up alone to the sound of the hotel manager on the phone. I think I can hear someone coming. Oh, no. That someone was a photographer. He just popped his head in the door and took a shot of me. I've got a horrible feeling the worst is yet to come . . .

June 23

5.00p.m.   *Channel Five*

'Soap Star Trashes Hotel.' My worst fears are confirmed. My photo is on the front page of the *Sydney Morning Courier*, complete with a graphic account of the party as described by several eyewitnesses. Needless to say, Casper is furious. This time I couldn't argue. Although it was not my fault, I have to concede this is bad publicity for the show and I do not look good. I assured Casper I would do my best to repair the damage, but even I had to admit there is not much I can do. Danny has made himself uncontactable, which doesn't surprise me. I blame him for a lot of this. I feel like killing him.

June 24

9.00p.m.   *Melanie's penthouse*

I finally had it out with Danny. I told him he is to blame for the damage to the hotel, as well as the irreparable damage to my reputation and bad publicity for the show. My mother is upset because of what she read in the paper, the other cast members are talking about me behind my back . . . the whole world is against me! To my surprise, Danny didn't deny the charge. Although he can't retract the bad press, he will reimburse me for the damage to the hotel and personally phone my parents and tell them he was responsible. He admits the drugs and alcohol got the better of him and promises not to allow anything like this to happen again. He told me he loves me . . . he doesn't want to lose me.

June 25

7.30p.m.   Melanie's penthouse

Danny has dropped a bombshell. His step-father is thinking about opening a couple of night clubs in Brisbane and wants Danny to go and look at potential venues. Danny has no choice but to obey. His step-father is quite annoyed at his distraction with Southern Cross Records. If Danny does him this favour he will earn enough brownie points to slack off again and concentrate on my music when he gets back. I'm not happy about this – especially since my life is in such turmoil – but there's nothing either of us can do. I suppose it's good in a way. We both need some time to ourselves.

June 26

7.30p.m.   *Channel Five*

I may have the solution to half of my problems. I have just returned from seeing Dennis, who put an incredible proposition to me. *Barossa Towers* is introducing a major new character, a super-bitch to stir up the show and stay for a long run. Dennis is a good friend of the producer and he suggested me for the part. Dennis feels I should turn my bad publicity into a positive. Like it or not, I have become one of the most infamous names in television and my image is suited perfectly to the role. What's more, *Barossa Towers* is a much more youth-orientated show. I would be wearing the latest clothes and playing a character much closer to the market for my music. It adds up to a very clever cross-promotion. I have to admit the offer sounds appealing. I have to get away from *Mercy Hospital*. I can't stand another day of the bitching, the crew and Casper. But there is still a big problem – I am under contract for several more months. Dennis, however, feels he can get round this. What does he have in mind?

June 27

7.30p.m.   *Melanie's penthouse*

I am leaving *Mercy Hospital*. Casper hauled me into his office and sat me down in the hot seat. I thought I was in trouble for something, but to my surprise, he was very pleasant and conciliatory. He had spoken to Dennis and agreed, all things considered, it would be best for me to leave the show. I was stunned. I never thought they would allow me to leave so easily. Casper's only request was that I say nothing about my departure. He will issue a press release and memo to the cast and crew. I have only four weeks left to go. The writers may not kill Sasha off. Instead, she might go on a short holiday and be replaced by another actress at a later date. I don't know how I feel – except numb. I wish Danny were here so we could talk about it.

June 28

5.00p.m.   Channel Five

I have received a two year contract for *Barossa Towers*. Dennis has negotiated a very attractive deal. I will be earning almost twice as much as I am on *Mercy Hospital*. I don't know much about my character, except that she is a bitch and it will be a very challenging role. *Barossa Towers* is getting a lot of press lately. They are tackling some very controversial storylines, so by all accounts this is a good move. I have to phone Danny in Brisbane.

June 29

12.00p.m.   Channel Five

Things are beginning to make sense. I asked Dennis how he managed to talk Casper into releasing me from *Mercy*

Hospital. I could tell he didn't want to answer, which made me even more curious. Finally, he admitted he had blackmailed him. He told him it would be in his interests to release me, otherwise he would blow the whistle on the advances he had made on female members of the cast. I was stunned. Though I am happy about joining *Barossa Towers,* I'm not sure I approve of the methods he took to get me there. Then again, Casper was the one who was at fault in the first place. He deserves to pay.

June 30

7.30p.m.   Melanie's penthouse

I spent today with Mum, Dad and Sebastian. I felt like a stranger. The only communication they have had with me over the past few weeks is through the media – they read about my antics in the hotel suite and my recording career. I haven't bothered to phone and tell them myself, let alone pay them a visit. They feel as though they are not part of my life. When they criticised my decision to leave *Mercy Hospital* I exploded. I told them they don't understand the industry and that I know what I am doing. Unfortunately, with hindsight, what they said makes a lot of sense. I do need to think long-term. I do need stability in my life. Changes are healthy, but running away is not. That's all I seem to do when the going gets tough: escape from one flat into another, jump from show to show. It's time the tough got tougher.

July 1

The word is out. The cast, crew and Sue-Ellen know I am leaving. However, they don't know I am joining *Barossa Towers* and I am not allowed to say anything until an official announcement is made. For this reason, they have all jumped to the conclusion I have been axed. Larissa came up to me in make-up and said 'Oh Melanie, I'm so sorry your going.' I know she means the opposite. David was genuinely upset. Despite our ups and downs I have grown to like David, and I'm ashamed I was so hard on him when we first worked together.

Dennis phoned me this afternoon to tell me Sue-Ellen had sent him a nasty fax. Sue-Ellen still receives ten per cent of my earnings from *Mercy Hospital*, so she is naturally upset by my premature departure. Dennis told me not to worry about it. Everything will be fine. I hope he is right.

July 2

I am fuming. Casper issued a press release about my departure. He worded it in such a way that it looks as though I have been fired by the show – because I am unprofessional and preoccupied with my music career! The sleaze bag! I have a good mind to ring *Exclusive* magazine and tell them the real reason he released me from my contract – because he made a pass at me! Dennis, however, advised me not to say anything. He assured me the press will soon know I am joining *Barossa Towers*, the rival soap, so it will be clear to everyone I had a better offer.

Danny is due back tomorrow. I can't wait to see him.

July 3

7.30p.m.   Charles Kingsford Smith Airport

I'm sitting at the airport, waiting to surprise Danny. I had the sense to wear a scarf and sunglasses, but this hasn't fooled anyone – I have been recognised at least a hundred times. A few people read about my 'axing' from the show and expressed their sympathy. I couldn't keep my mouth shut. I told them that I hadn't been axed and that I am working on an exciting new project. Right now, a bunch of soccer players are staring at me. I wish Danny's plane would hurry up and get here!

July 4

4.20p.m.   Channel Five

Danny's plane never arrived. I got home at eleven last night after waiting for every flight from Brisbane in the hope he would be on one of them. His mobile was turned off and he wasn't at his hotel, so I assumed he was in transit. When I got home I found a message from him on the answering machine simply saying his business had been extended. He didn't even say he'd read the bad press or ask what was happening. Now he won't be home for another couple of days. I'm really annoyed.

July 5

12.30p.m.   Channel Five

I feel like a Russian spy! I had breakfast with Pierce Rogers, the producer of *Barossa Towers*. We met at his production office, as I can't be seen anywhere near Channel Eleven, where *Barossa Towers* is actually filmed, until I'm finished on *Mercy Hospital*. Pierce is quite young, on my wavelength. He has watched my progress on *Mercy* and feels I will be a huge asset to his show. We talked about my character, Jessie Wells. She turns out to be a schizophrenic in the first week! I told Pierce I was quite nervous about handling the material, especially as I have no preparation time between finishing on *Mercy* and starting on *Barossa*. He assured me I would be fine. I hope so!

July 6 & 7

7.45p.m.   Melanie's penthouse

Alone in the penthouse . . . This weekend has flown by, just like every other. I spent most of today answering fan mail, which dates back to the beginning of the year. I'm only beginning to realise what an impact Sasha has had on viewers. The loss of her close friend in a car accident struck a particular chord. Lots of young girls have written in to share similar experiences and ask my advice. Tamara opens all the mail before I receive it and has already sent out some pamphlets on bereavement, but I feel I owe them a personal reply. I still have a mountain of mail – I guess it will have to wait until next weekend. I hope Danny is back by then.

July 8

10.00p.m.   Melanie's penthouse

I try so hard to be angry with Danny, but somehow he always manages to win me over. He finally phoned and told me he was coming home in a couple of days. He also told me Wire had finished editing the video clip and had organised a screening next weekend. The Southern Cross Records executives want to see the result, then they will start talking about a release date. This will probably coincide with my screen debut on *Barossa Towers*. There is so much to think about!

July 9

4.30p.m.   Channel Five

Today is never-ending. I have thirteen scenes, mostly with Larissa and David. The latest storyline has Sasha finding out that their characters are together. I don't think all is well between Larissa and David. She is doing everything she can to get publicity, talking about their private life and also making references to my past 'relationship' with David. Despite this, she is proving to be very popular and is getting a lot of fan mail. If only the public knew what she was really like!

July 10

7.30p.m.   Melanie's penthouse

Nothing remains a secret in television. The *Sydney Morning Courier* has run the story on my move to *Barossa Towers*, under the headline, 'Soap Star Jumps Sinking Ship'. The details are very accurate, describing the terms of my new contract and details of my new character. The cast and crew have mixed reactions. Larissa, of course, is fuming. While she's happy I'm off the show, she doesn't like the idea of me going to something better. She even hinted that the show's ratings were falling. David was happy for me, though he admitted he would miss me a great deal.

Brad's reaction was the most chilling. He, too, was offered a role on *Barossa Towers* but didn't take it. He warned me it is very dangerous to swap shows, especially when they are on rival networks. The political situation is a minefield. The Channel Five executives won't be happy. They have invested a lot of money turning me into a star. They've also put a lot of effort into turning my bad press into good press, when it would have been easier for them to cut their losses and get rid of me ages ago. Now another network stands to reap the benefits. When I leave I will be sure to thank them personally for all they have done for me. The bottom line is, however, that I was made a better offer. If they ask any more questions I will simply divert them to Casper for the real story. I wonder what they'd think of that!

July 11

8.00p.m.   Melanie's penthouse

Danny is home! I have forgotten all of my anger, frustration and despair. I am so happy to see him. I'm not going to write any more – we are going to enjoy our night together. Later.

July 12

9.00p.m.   Melanie's penthouse

My life is in turmoil! I arrived home to find my scripts for *Barossa Towers*, which I am going to have to learn while wrapping up my final weeks on *Mercy*. There is more coverage in the papers, with columnists speculating on my decision to switch shows – they're not sure it's a good one. I'm not going to think about any of it now – the video screening is tomorrow night. Danny is planning a party. If the Southern Cross executives are happy they will set a date for the release of the record, which spells out more work and stress for me. There is also my lingering fear that the press will find out it isn't really me on the record. If this comes out I'll be history!

July 13 & 14 & 15

3.30p.m.   Botany Bay Hospital

I'm lucky to be alive. I'm at the location for *Mercy Hospital* – but this time I really am lying in a bed. I'm slowly pasting together the events of the last few days. The video launch was a disaster. The clip was the most bizarre clash of images I have ever seen. The executives hated it. They told Danny it would have to be re-shot, costing thousands of dollars the company doesn't have. To make matters worse, Marcia Love was busy telling everyone that not only does she dance in the video but that she is the lead vocalist too, and that I couldn't sing. I was a complete laughing stock. I told Danny we had to get out of there.

We went on to PMT, where I ran into some of the cast of *Barossa Towers*. I'd had a bit to drink and decided to introduce myself, given we will be working together in a couple of weeks. They didn't want to know me. They are not happy about me coming on to the show, especially as I am getting paid a lot of money and my character is apparently at the forefront of the storylines. There I was thinking I was walking into a bright, happy environment – but it sounds like an even bitchier set-up than *Mercy*.

Back home, Danny did something unforgivable: again

he tried to get me to take a line of coke. He said it would blow my troubles away. I was tempted, but I've seen what it does to him. I hate Danny when he's high and I hated him for suggesting that I get high. I had to get away. I hopped into my car and whizzed down the road, but I didn't make it past the first turn. I lost control of the wheel and swerved into a telegraph pole. Then I passed out.

I woke up a few hours ago to find my mother at my bedside. She was in tears. Apparently Danny was here. Mum and Dad told him to leave. They blame him for all of this. I know Danny has his bad points, but he is not really to blame. I have to see him. I have to hear him say everything is going to be all right.

July 16

6.30p.m.   Botany Bay Hospital

I have been asleep for most of the day. My room is full of flowers, most of them sent by fans who read about my accident in the paper. I haven't seen any of the press but I know it can't be good. The police did a test for drugs and alcohol and found I was way over the limit on alcohol, which means I can kiss my driving licence goodbye. I may also have to appear in court and pay a fine. My car is a write-off. I suppose I should be thankful I escaped with cuts and bruises – nothing make-up can't fix. But I'm terribly shaken.

Mercy Hospital has rescheduled all my scenes. I can see the crew outside the window. Some tried to come up but I told the duty nurse I didn't want any visitors. Except Danny. He came by this morning but I was asleep. I still haven't seen him.

July 17

3.30p.m.   Botany Bay Hospital

I have seen Danny – maybe for the last time. He bought me a big bunch of flowers. I thought he was going to sympathise, feel some remorse about the accident and promise to look after me. But he said none of those things. He made a joke of it, recalling some incident where he almost crashed while he was on drugs. I sat there, listening, incredulous. I did crash! I could have been killed! And killed other innocent people! But he didn't care. As far as he's concerned, it didn't happen so there is no point in worrying about it.

For the first time everything has become clear. I have been living on borrowed time, breaking all the rules. But life is not a game. When it's over you can't turn the board and play again. You can't expect to role a dice and jump three places without stepping on people along the way. That's what we've been doing. And look where I've landed. In a hospital bed! I told him to get out. I love Danny . . . but after this, how can I believe he loves me?

July 18 & 19

6.30p.m.   Mosman Manor

It feels great to be home. My parents insisted I recover at their place, away from Danny and the show. Next week is my final week on *Mercy Hospital*. Not only will this be difficult as my character does her goodbye rounds, but all my scenes from this week have been rescheduled for then so my workload is effectively double. I don't think I will be well enough but I have no choice.

Against Mum and Dad's wishes I'm going back to the penthouse tomorrow. I have thought long and hard about my future with Danny. I can't forgive him for taking such a callous attitude to my accident. The problem is I love him. I don't think anyone else has ever loved him – parents, friends or other family – and this is what he needs. He is a lost soul and needs help. It will be hard, but if he's willing, I will be there every step of the way. Then, with a clean slate, maybe we can have some future together.

July 20 & 21

6.30p.m.   Mosman Jetty

I haven't been able to face anyone. Not my parents, not myself . . . not even you. I never want to see Danny as long as I live. I returned to the penthouse determined to start anew and salvage our relationship. Danny was in his room, but he wasn't alone. He was with Marcia Love. He is having an affair with her! I feel cheap, used, played for a fool. It must have started when we were recording, probably that night I surprised him and she was there. All those nights Danny was working late, all the time he was supposedly in Brisbane – how do I know he wasn't with Marcia? Danny didn't try to deny it. He didn't even apologise. This is the final straw. He's obviously determined to keep living hard and fast. If he won't accept my help, there's nothing more I can do. He even offered to return the ring I bought him, but I told him to keep it. I want nothing from him.

I am back at my parents' house, though I haven't told them the full story. I have spent most of today on this jetty, the place where I used to sit and dream about being famous. I thought it would bring me happiness . . . but so far, it has brought me nothing but misery.

July 22

7.00p.m.   Melanie's penthouse

Out with the old . . . well, almost. This week is one of transition. I have just five more days on *Mercy Hospital*, by which time the memory of Danny should be erased from my mind. Well, that's the plan. I came home to find the penthouse empty. I packed up all Danny's belongings and left them downstairs, along with a note about how he can arrange to pick up his furniture. He'll have to organise a time with the landlord as I don't want to see him again.

The process is painful, but it is one that has to be done if I am to cope with what is ahead of me. There is still the record, despite the fact that the video is a disaster. I have a deal and will have to fulfil my contractual obligations. I'm not exactly thrilled about having to mime Marcia's words, but I'm not going to let her ruin it for me. I'm never touching booze again. I know how destructive it is. I could have died because of drink and, as for Danny, well his time may come sooner than he thinks.

July 23

5.00p.m.   Channel Five

I thought today was going to be terrible. Everyone knows about my accident and has the right to be angry for the trouble I have caused, but I was surprised by their sympathy. David welcomed me with a hug. Billy was practically in tears as he applied make-up to my healing wounds. Despite all the times I have been late and he has had to rush me on to the set, Billy has a soft spot for me. Angie also got a jolt into reality. While my accident was casued by excess alcohol, her drug addiction is potentially more dangerous – her luck is going to run out. I had no hesitation in telling her this. Larissa, however, was her usual snide self. To add insult to injury, she has appointed herself chief organiser of my going away party. This is one party where I'm not going to lose control of myself.

I'm not even going to have one glass of champagne. This is the new me.

July 24

11.00p.m.   Melanie's penthouse

I'm about to fall into bed . . . except I don't have one any more. Danny still hasn't picked up his furniture, though his personal items have disappeared from downstairs – maybe someone decided to help themselves. I have had eighteen scenes today. I have just as many tomorrow. I have to sleep!

July 25

10.00p.m.   Channel Five

I don't think I'm going to survive this week. I got a call from the landlord today. Danny has picked up his furniture. He hasn't bothered to call me. I wouldn't speak to him anyway, but I thought he would at least try. I can't believe it is over.

July 26

9.00p.m.   Melanie's penthouse

I'm home at a decent hour, but there is a catch – I have to start at five tomorrow morning! My last day on *Mercy Hospital* will be a killer. Sixteen scenes! Then I have my going away party, which Larissa has organised at a Chinese restaurant. She knows I hate Chinese! Danny has taken all his furniture, but he hasn't left what I want to remember him by – a cheque to cover his rent and the damage to the hotel suite, which is stacking up on my credit card. This means I am going to have to phone him. I'm not looking forward to it.

July 27 & 28

5.00p.m.   Melanie's penthouse

I can't blame it on alcohol or drugs . . . I can't blame it on anything. Last night, after my going away party, I brought someone home – David. We kissed. I can't remember how or why it happened. I only remember crying and David comforting me. I remember feeling as though a chapter of my life was closing, yet I had so many regrets and things I wanted to change. He was there to comfort me, assure me everything would be fine, assure me I am a good person. I'm just as beautiful on the inside as I am on the outside. Then it happened. He took me in his arms, one thing led to another . . .

July 29

3.30p.m.   Bondi Beach

I have spent today incognito on the beach, reading my scripts for *Barossa Towers*. It is a beautiful winter's day and I am soaking up the sun. The more I get into Jessie Wells, the more I can relate to her schizophrenic behaviour ... God knows, I feel as though I am living multiple lives at the moment! The pace of the show is entirely different. While *Mercy Hospital* is very slow and regimented in style, *Barossa Towers* is far more adventurous. There is always something happening, though I must admit the writers sometimes go a little too far. I'm nervous about tomorrow, especially as I know some of the actors don't like me. But I'm going to make it work.

July 30

7.30p.m.   Melanie's penthouse

I've just skimmed over my entry on November 30 last year, my first day on *Mercy Hospital*. I was overwhelmed by the experience, everything was new and exciting. I didn't have those feelings on *Barossa Towers* today. Although I hadn't met the people, I knew what their jobs were and I didn't have to ask a thousand questions. I had only one scene today, at the location where Jessie lives. The director is very young. He wasn't concerned with my performance, but rather with framing the shot and turning the background scenery into some kind of art form. There were no other actors in the scene, just voice overs which will be added when the scene is edited. Jessie has lots of scenes on her own where she hears voices. This is hard for me to act, as I'm basically reacting to silence and talking to myself. I think I did a good job. Nobody told me otherwise.

July 31

7.30p.m.   Channel Eleven

I feel lost. As though I am on a desert island with all my provisions but no one to talk to. The *Barossa Towers* green room is always empty. David rang this morning to see how I am getting along. We never said anything about the other night. He was very awkward on the phone. I'm not sure how he feels about me now, but my feelings for him haven't changed. He was a friend and he was there when I needed him. He, too, needed me. If anybody took advantage of anybody, we both did it to each other.

August 1

7.30p.m.   Melanie's penthouse

I didn't know snakes could walk, but Marcia Love's venomous tongue sure knows how to travel. I was hauled into Southern Cross Records this morning to talk about the state of my musical career, which has basically been in limbo for the last couple of weeks. Lex, who produced the record in the first place, is keen to do something with it despite Danny and Wire's botched job of the video clip. He didn't say what he has in mind. He just wanted to talk to me about it. I told him I was keen to go on with it but that I must have input into the video clip and control of my image. I can't afford to make another mistake. Lex didn't say much, except that he would be in touch when Southern Cross had made up their minds about what to do.

As I was leaving, Marcia Love slithered in. She made a point of telling me that she and Danny are still seeing each other and, for my information, they had been for some time before Danny and I broke up. She said they used to laugh about me when they were together. Danny always thought she was number one – I was second best! I held myself together, turned on my heels and left. But as soon as I walked out the door, I lost my composure. It shouldn't hurt, but it does. Not because I still love Danny . . . but because I made such a fool of myself.

August 2

6.00p.m.   Channel Eleven

I got a nice surprise when I arrived at the studio today – a dressing-room with my name on the door! The studio is quite empty, contrasting with the hustle and bustle of Channel Five. There is only one other lifestyle show in production, which shoots a couple of days a week, so there isn't the constant parade of famous faces like there was at Channel Five. All in all, the atmosphere is very different. And as all my scenes have been on my own, I haven't had

much chance to meet the other cast. I guess I will. I hope
I like them.

August 3

2.30p.m.   Melanie's penthouse

I've just opened a letter from the bank. I've been receiving
them for weeks, but for fear of the contents I have let
them slip. I can no longer ignore my ten thousand dollar
overdraft. Most of this is Danny's debt – damage to the
hotel room, mobile phone bills which he put on my card
unbeknown to me, as well as other purchases he talked
me into. He promised to cover this. I'm going to have to
make sure he does.

August 4

3.30p.m.   McKillop Street

I'm on location. *Barossa Towers* is actually a dilapidated
old apartment block, nothing like it appears on screen.
I've driven past a few times and not even noticed it. I'm
doing my first scene with Andre. My character, Jessie, is
moving in with his character, Michael. Andre made some
sleazy joke about my breasts, a chilling hint of sexual
harassment to come. To think I actually used to idolise
this guy!

August 5

My workload is speeding up. The latest batch of scripts
has Jessie interacting with more of the other characters. I
heard a rumour Desiree was auditioning for a part. I hope
she gets it. I rang Danny's mobile this morning, but every
time I get hold of him the line mysteriously falls out. I
have left a couple of messages at PMT and Firecracker,
telling him to get back to me. I'm sure he knows this is
about money. He's not getting away without paying me.

August 6

7.30p.m.   *Melanie's penthouse*

I feel like I'm back on *Mercy Hospital*. Today has been
exhausting, my first hard schedule since I started on this
show. I had four scenes in studio, all with Andre. One of
them was a fantasy sequence, where one of Jessie's multiple
personalities hallucinates about knowing Michael in a past
life. The studio was full of smoke which nearly made me
choke. Then I had to kiss Andre, which definitely made
me choke – he put his tongue so far down my throat I
could hardly breathe! Tomorrow I have to shoot the title
sequence and publicity shots for my fan card. Another
big day. I hope I find the time to answer a call from Danny.

August 7

I've finally got a new bed. The owner of the furniture store is a huge fan of *Mercy Hospital* so I autographed a pillow-case and he gave me a discount! I told him I was now on *Barossa Towers*, but he didn't take very kindly to this. He thinks the storylines on *Barossa Towers* are far-fetched and he no longer allows his family to watch the show. I know what he means.

We shot the title sequence this morning. The cast of *Barossa* are credited at the beginning of the show, as opposed to the end like *Mercy*. I shot my piece from a skyscraper, as if Jessie is about to jump – I hope it doesn't look as ridiculous as it felt!

August 8

5.00p.m.   *Channel Eleven*

I still haven't heard from Danny. I don't want to see him, but if I want the money, I have no choice. I'm working late tonight but have a late start tomorrow morning, the perfect opportunity to pay him a visit.

August 9

7.30p.m.   *Melanie's penthouse*

I am fuming. I popped over to Danny's parents this

morning, only to find out that he never moved back home. He left my place and moved straight in with Marcia! His parents refused to pass on any message to him, saying they were sick and tired of my childish antics and want nothing to do with me. Can you believe it?

August 10

12.00p.m.   *Channel Eleven*

'Star Couple Split'. I got a shock when I saw David and Larissa on the cover. I haven't heard from David for a few days so I naturally assumed he'd put our fling behind him and resolved things with Larissa. However, according to the story, the official line is work pressures but I could tell David's quotes actually referred to me. He phoned this morning, but I didn't have time to talk. I don't have the energy to call him back. I'm worried about what he has to say.

August 11

9.00p.m.   *Melanie's penthouse*

I've just closed the door on David. Just as Danny has broken my heart, I think I have shattered his into a thousand pieces. He told me he is in love with me. While he understands our night together was impulsive on my behalf, he thinks there is enough chemistry between us to at least make a go of things. This feels so strange! Six months ago we were pretending to be a couple. After all our efforts to make a public split, he now wants us to get together! I told him I valued his friendship, but I am still getting over Danny and I'm not ready for another commitment. He was disappointed, but he accepted this. He's a really nice guy.

August 12

6.30p.m.   Channel Eleven

My life is such a soap opera. Just when I thought I'd heard the last of the David saga, I now cop the brunt of Larissa's bruised ego. I saw her this afternoon at an AIDS charity luncheon where we were stuck sitting at the same table. Every time she picked up her knife I could tell she wanted to put it through my back, but she saved any sign of hostility until we were alone in the toilets. She told me she knew about David and me. She said she wouldn't waste her energy exacting revenge. I'm doing a good enough job messing up my own career! I held my composure, but her words struck a raw nerve. Although I don't like Larissa, I have done to her what Marcia Love did to me – so what does that make me?

August 13

3.30p.m.   McKillop Street

I've just had a meeting with my accountant, Gerard. I was

anticipating a huge tax return, but I can't actually claim a lot of my expenses – as it turns out, most of them were Danny's. I'm also having an argument with my car insurance company, who say I am not covered for the accident. I paid my insurance beforehand, but evidently the cheque bounced and as no money was actually received, they refuse to pay for the damage. In the meantime, I have to get cabs to and from work as this was not part of the *Barossa Towers* deal. Until I catch up with Danny, I'm going to ask Dennis to get me as many personal appearances as possible. I need to make some fast cash.

August 14

10.00p.m.   Melanie's penthouse

I wish I'd never met Danny. I phoned Dennis this morning begging him to secure me some night club appearances. It seems Danny has sabotaged my reputation, discouraging managers from booking me by telling them I am unprofessional. This, accompanied with my bad press, has been enough to send them running. Danny has done so much to hurt me . . . why is he twisting the knife?

August 15 & 16

5.00p.m.   Channel Eleven

Busy, busy, busy. I have hardly had a minute to myself over the last couple of days. To make matters worse,

Channel Eleven have ordered massive rewrites on some upcoming storylines involving Jessie. They feel the schizophrenic storyline is unrealistic and, although nobody has actually said it, I don't think they're happy with my performance. I doubt whether Meryl Streep could do a good job of this material.

August 17

8.00p.m.   Melanie's penthouse

I used to look forward to coming home. Now there is just emptiness. I'm going to have to change my phone number yet again. There are all these crank messages on the answerphone but, unfortunately, there is nothing from Danny. I have no choice but to go looking for him. There is a major launch at PMT tomorrow night. I'm sure he'll be there. I'll confront him.

August 18

Midnight   Melanie's penthouse

I'm still shaking. I stormed into PMT, armed with a stack of bills and more than a few words to say to Danny. I found him by the bar with Marcia hanging by his side. The entire club was staring at us. There has been a few remarks in the press about our break-up, especially around the time of my accident. Everyone knows the situation. Keen to avoid a scene, Danny led me out the back and practically threw me up against a wall. I never knew he was violent, but he was obviously off his face so this no doubt contributed to his anger. He ripped into me for embarrassing him in front of his friends and began to throw things around. I was terrified. Then, like one of Jessie's personalities, he did a complete turnaround and tried to kiss me. I managed to push him away and made a quick escape, bowling over Marcia who was waiting outside the door. Danny is a speeding car. How much longer before he crashes?

August 19 & 20

7.00p.m.   Adelaide Hotel

Somebody should plant a bomb under this town. No, not really. I didn't start out with a good attitude, given this publicity trip was a last minute idea and I had to cancel all my other plans. Then I find we are staying in a shonky three star hotel right underneath a flight path! Then, during a shopping centre appearance, I was pelted with a rotten tomato. There were plenty of photographers on hand so no doubt it will be in tomorrow's paper. Some guy has also been following me around, but Andre has been there to protect me – with his hand creeping towards my breast. Our flight has been delayed another hour. I have this horrible feeling of drowning, a bit like when things got too much on *Mercy Hospital*. This time I'm not going to let it happen. When the flight attendant tells us

196

our life jacket is under our seats, I'm going to grab it –
never know when it will come in handy.

August 21

4.30p.m.   Channel Eleven

I did an interview today, my first in ages. I met the
journalist way back when I started on *Mercy Hospital*. She
commented on how much I had changed. She said I looked
much older, but I don't think this was a compliment – the
stress and pressure are taking a mean toll. She asked me
about 'I Know You Want Me'. I couldn't tell her when it
was being released, though I gave the impression it is still
going ahead. I'll have to pay Southern Cross Records a visit.

August 22

8.30p.m.   Melanie's penthouse

My recording career is over. I went into Southern Cross
Records and talked to Lex. After much stepping around
the subject, I finally got him to admit the executives have
had a change of heart – they are pulling the plug on the
record. The official line is lack of finances but I'm sure
the real reason is me. As much as I've tried to deny it, I
can't sing so there really isn't any point. And my public
image is so tarnished they can't afford to take a risk. I'm
beginning to wonder if anything else can possibly go
wrong.

August 23

I can hardly keep my eyes open. Mum, Dad and Sebastian came over tonight. I haven't seen them in weeks. Mum cooked a casserole and left it in the fridge. They wanted to stay longer, but I am so exhausted I had to ask them to leave so I could get some sleep. I feel terrible – I never get to see them.

August 24

Midnight   *Melanie's penthouse*

Last night I couldn't stop myself from falling asleep – tonight I can't get to sleep. Insomnia is a recurring problem for me, no doubt brought on by stress. I have a stack of fan mail from *Mercy Hospital*, so I think I might answer some letters. I can feel massive bags forming under my eyes . . .

August 25

3.00p.m.   *Bondi Beach*

I didn't sleep a wink last night. I had to take caffeine tablets to maintain my energy at work. They have had the effect of hyping me up even more. I'm now at the beach, hoping the fresh air will temper my anxiety and help me to chill out. People are looking at me. I'm finally on air with *Barossa Towers* next week. I'm looking forward to people recognising me as Jessie. I want to put Sasha behind me.

August 26

3.00p.m.   Channel Eleven

I'm sitting in the canteen. The atmosphere is dull and lifeless. The traffic consists of office workers, not the celebrity faces I used to see at Channel Five. I'm finding it hard to decipher the latest batch of scripts. Jessie's condition is coming to a head. She is admitted to a mental institution! I told Pierce I wasn't confident about handling it, so he suggested I do some research. Of course, an *Exclusive* photographer has been invited along for the ride. I hardly slept last night either, so I'd better get some rest tonight – tomorrow will be a big day.

August 27

7.30p.m.   Melanie's penthouse

Today taught me a lot about myself. I went to the mental institution, along with a make-up artist and the *Exclusive* photographer. The predicament of the residents was upsetting but the photographer was far more interested in framing me for shots. I had a couple of wardrobe swaps and had to change in a supply room. As I was slipping into another sweater, I noticed I wasn't alone – a chest full of sleeping tablets was staring me in the face! The answer to my insomnia. It would have been so easy to pocket a packet, but I defied temptation. I'm going to force myself to get a good night's sleep tonight.

Listen to me patting myself on the back for not stealing the tablets; I spent the whole day with people who have problems far worse than I could ever imagine. I don't know the meaning of hardship.

August 28

6.35p.m.   *Channel Eleven*

I've just committed a cardinal sin – I watched another channel. I have a couple of hours between scenes so I thought I'd check out *Mercy Hospital*. Even though I have left, I forget their lives are going on. Larissa and David are now together on screen, which I'm sure is difficult as they have split in real life. I'm half-tempted to ring David, just to talk, but I'm worried he'll get the wrong idea. Andre has just walked in. He's coming my way – so I'll put you away!

August 29

5.00p.m.   *Melanie's penthouse*

Bills, bills and more bills. But still no money from Danny. I guess I have to face the fact that I'll never get anything from him. He has bled me completely dry. I'm going to have to budget. No more new clothes for the next week!

August 30

6.30p.m.   *Channel Eleven*

This industry is full of sleaze bags. Andre sneaked into my dressing-room and groped me from behind. I turned round and slapped him across the face. He's now in make-up, trying to cover the red handprint I left in my wake. This is history repeating itself, though this time it is much worse. At least Casper knew when to take a hint. Andre, however, is an oversexed lech!

August 31

10.00p.m.   *Melanie's penthouse*

Tonight I celebrated my on air debut on *Barossa Towers* – all alone. Mum and Dad invited me over, but I had a late finish and didn't feel like company. I'm not sure what to make of my new role. Jessie has a lot more depth than Sasha, but the material is borderline – I'm on a tight-rope teetering between being plausible and looking completely stupid. I wonder if Danny is watching.

September 1

3.30p.m.   *Waratah Valley*

We are back at the mental institution. This is the second

time I have been here and I'm feeling more and more like a patient! It's quite sobering to meet the residents again – their problems put mine into perspective.

I got some interesting feedback from the cab driver on the way to work this morning. He said he hadn't watched *Barossa Towers* for weeks, but he tuned in last night and I happened to be on. He thought I was terrific!

September 2

3.30p.m.   *Melanie's penthouse*

This is the final straw. I had to go back to Southern Cross Records today and sign a few papers, mere formalities to null and void my recording deal. Who should be there but Marcia Love – putting her signature on a long term contract! She wasted no time telling me what the first single will be: 'I Know You Want Me'. According to Marcia, Lex was so impressed with her vocals (not to mention the fact that she's a six-foot tart), he wants to make her a huge star. She started talking about how wonderfully supportive Danny has been. I couldn't take it any more. I turned my back on her – and went straight into a supermarket where I bought a huge block of chocolate! Suffice to say, there isn't any left!

September 3

This is a dark day in the history of television. Jobs are on the line and no one seems sure what will happen to *Barossa Towers*. Larissa was right after all – the ratings don't look good.

I phoned Dennis straight away. He assured me they cannot cut my wage. I would be in big trouble if they did. I have worked out a six-month plan to pay off my debts and I need every cent I earn. I told Dennis to have another go at securing me some night club appearances. Hopefully Danny has stopped bad-mouthing me so I can finally get some work.

September 4

I've just read my first review for *Barossa Towers*. The critic wasn't very kind. He wasn't so much putting down my performance as the storyline which is very controversial for its time slot. The ratings have also dropped a couple of points. This happened on *Mercy Hospital* and everyone panicked, but that show is still around to tell the story. I'm sure we'll be fine.

September 5

The smell of death is in the air. Huge job cuts were announced today. They are cutting back on all the support staff – wardrobe assistants, runners, the little people. Pierce called to confirm the cuts, but assured the rest of us our jobs were fine. Recent storylines have attracted bad press, but he is confident ratings will rise again. I think there will be more changes.

September 6

8.00p.m.   *Melanie's penthouse*

I'm having an early night. I'm still suffering from insomnia, but I figure going to bed earlier gives me more hope of a full night's sleep. Later.

September 7

12.00p.m.   *Melanie's penthouse*

I'm in a state of shock. Pierce has just called me with the news: *Barossa Towers* has been axed! We will continue to shoot until the end of the week, but then it is over. The official line is falling ratings, but the rumour is the network has a better show in the pipeline. Apparently the network wants to change its image and target a new audience. I can't believe it. I quit *Mercy Hospital* to join this show;

now, one month into the job, I'm out of work. I know I should be on the phone to Dennis, working out what to do next – but all I want to do is shut the world out. I don't want to think about my unpaid bills, the public humiliation – I just want to believe everything will be fine.

September 8

4.00p.m.   *Channel Eleven*

I feel like the walking dead. The studio floor is silent, except for the actors reading their lines. There are no jokes from the crew, no hustle and bustle. I went to see Dennis this morning. He assured me everything would be fine. He admitted this was a hiccup in my three year plan, but he would steer me in another direction and I would be back on my feet in no time. He's a reputable agent so I trust him. I have no other choice.

September 9 & 10 & 11

6.30p.m.   *Melanie's penthouse*

The show is over. I didn't come home until late last night as I went to the *Barossa Towers* wrap party. My final day on set was strange. I'd only been on the show for a few weeks, so I didn't feel the same sense of loss as some of the other actors. Mine was less sentimental and more financial. I actually talked to more of the cast last night than I have in all the time I've been on the show. Most were shocked. It was only this year *Barossa Towers* won the *Exclusive* Magazine award for most popular drama, beating other shows which are still on the air. This just goes to prove how fickle this business is.

The wrap party was a budget affair. They showed a goof reel which included one of my blunders – I had an awful time fitting into that straight jacket! Afterwards, many of the cast went to PMT. I didn't want to go. I knew Danny would be there. I walked out of the studio with a bagful of Jessie's wardrobe and came home. I slept through to midday today.

I'm going to visit the family tomorrow then on Monday, start doing the rounds – time to get my career back on track.

September 12

8.30p.m.   Melanie's penthouse

Family. Can't live with them, can't live without them. Mum and Dad put on a barbecue, doing their best to take my mind off my unemployment and make it seem just like old times. Problem is, it was! I felt as though I hadn't made any progress at all. Mum and Dad suggested I move back home, but this made me feel worse – I don't want to concede defeat. Besides, Dennis said he would look after me. I have no reason to doubt him.

September 13

5.00p.m.   Melanie's penthouse

I spent all morning waiting for the phone to ring. I left three messages with Dennis, but he didn't return any of them so I marched in to see him. I had to sit in reception for more than an hour, while young hopefuls without a minute's experience commanded more of his time. Finally, I got to see him. The everything-will-be-fine bravado from last week had gone. Dennis checked in his book and noted me down for a casting. I nearly died when he told me what it was for – a bit-part in a corporate video. There's no way I'm going to lower myself for that kind of work. I told Dennis I'd wait until something substantial came up.

September 14 & 15

8.30p.m.   Melanie's penthouse

The phone still hasn't rung. I'm going to bed.

September 16

4.00p.m.   Bondi Beach

The phone finally rang. It was my estate agent. My rent is one month overdue. A quick stop by the autobank indicates I barely have the money to pay. I've finally got my car fixed and by the time I pay for the repairs, I'll have practically nothing left. There is no point worrying. I'll pay the rent. Something will come up. I'm sure of it. Until then, I'm going to make use of the spring weather and polish my tan. I hope these storm clouds go the other way.

September 17

7.30p.m.   *Melanie's penthouse*

I'm never going out the door again. I went to the supermarket today and got accosted by every single passerby. One woman had the nerve to go through my trolley. Upon seeing my cheap label purchases, she made some comment about me being all washed up. To make matters worse, Larissa is on the front cover of *Exclusive*. It used to be me! I wish she'd go back to Scotland.

September 18

8.30p.m.   *Melanie's penthouse*

I woke up this morning ready to take on the world. I decided I may as well go for whatever castings are available, just to make ends meet until the next job comes along. I phoned Dennis and asked for the details. The corporate video audition is tomorrow. I may as well go for it.

September 19

I knew I shouldn't have lowered myself! I was just about to go into the casting agency, when who should I bump into coming out of the building but Marcia! I could tell she was embarrassed and that she was wondering how to cover the fact she was there. She gave me a weak smile and told me she was dashing off to an appointment. What's the betting she's split up with Danny and her record deal is off? Well, I certainly wasn't going to the audition after that encounter.

September 20

3.30p.m.   *Melanie's penthouse*

I know it has only been days, but I feel as though I haven't worked for months. Looking back over this diary, I used to complain about my workload all the time. Now I'd give anything to be back on a show. Wait. Maybe I can. I have an idea.

September 21

8.45p.m.   *Melanie's penthouse*

I bit the bullet and phoned Casper at *Mercy Hospital*. He was surprised to hear from me, but within seconds, knew the reason I was calling. I asked for my old job back. I promised five hundred per cent commitment. I even suggested a way for Sasha to return to the show, albeit a rehash of a *Barossa Towers* plot. He cut me dead. He reminded me that they were thinking about recasting the role with another actress and had no interest in having me back. He wished me luck for the future . . . then hung up. I am going to cry.

September 22

6.00p.m.   Melanie's penthouse

My life is going downhill. My hand is trembling. It has been ever since I picked up the phone and Dennis blasted the hell out of me. He heard on the grapevine that I had asked Casper for my old job back. He said this severely undermined my faith in him, especially as he pulled such elaborate strings to get me off *Mercy Hospital* in the first place. I tried to reason with him but, before I could say any more, he dropped me from the agency. An hour later my file was returned to me. I have no job, no agent . . . do I have a future at all?

September 23

7.30p.m.   Melanie's penthouse

I must have talked to every agent in Sydney today. Their books are either shut or they're not interested – either way I have no hope of landing representation. On top of this, I received my latest mobile phone bill. I owe for the last three months and if I don't pay within seven days, my line will be disconnected. I can't afford to lose my phone. It is my lifeline.

September 24

8.00p.m.   Melanie's penthouse

I'd offer you somewhere to sit but I'm afraid I no longer have a couch. I put an advertisement on the window of the corner shop and found a buyer straight away. They came over to pick it up. To my horror, they were die-hard soap fans. They wanted to know what I was up to now. I made up some elaborate story about having many irons in the fire. I also let on that I had an even better lounge suite on the way, the only reason I was getting rid of this one. I have made enough money to cover the mobile phone bill, but not much more.

September 25

7.30p.m.   Melanie's penthouse

I have just received an eviction notice. I thought I'd covered the rent, but evidently one of the cheques bounced (yet again) and I still owe more. I have one last resort. I'll tell you about it tomorrow.

September 26

I have hit rock bottom. I have just survived the most humiliating experience of my life. I drove myself down to social security, determined to enrol for unemployment benefits. I parked out the front for three hours. There was a television news crew inside, no doubt reporting on the latest unemployment figures. I couldn't risk being caught on the evening news. They finally disappeared and I plucked up the courage to go in. The lighting was so dim I had to take off my sunglasses, which revealed my true identity – much to the delight of a crowd of school-leavers. They couldn't believe their favourite TV star was lining up to get the dole! They even asked to have their photograph taken with me. Unable to confess the truth, I said I was there to research a part. I don't think any of them believed me. I couldn't bear to hang around any longer, so I left . . . without even claiming a cent.

September 27

What goes around comes around. I'm coming around. I'm sitting at Pietro's Cafe, the place where I worked my butt off and dreamed of a career in television. I have been there, done that – now I'm right back where I started. Pietro came over and asked me how I was. For the first time in my life I was completely honest. I told him I had lost it all. And I have. I'm looking out on to the beach, where a year ago this roller-coaster began when I won Miss Bondi. Maxwell McKenzie has reminded me I am committed to crowning the new Miss Bondi in four weeks time. I hope I can bring myself to do it. I know I will give the winner much better advice than I have followed. If I could do it all again, I would do it very differently. I would – I don't believe it. There is Troy . . . and Nadine is on his arm. Too late. He has seen me. He's not wearing his pizza uniform and he's getting into a new car. I'm looking away . . . I don't want him to see the tears in my eyes.

10.00p.m.   Melanie's penthouse

I have nothing left to live for. I am a horrible person. I have been horrible to my family. I have been horrible to Troy – yet he was the only person who truly loved me. I wasted the fantastic opportunity of a career, all for the love of someone who used and abused me. Danny. He taught me so much but left me feeling as though I had so little. The worst thing is, I still love him. Yes, as much as I have tried to deny it, I do. But that love only makes me hate myself. I think everyone else does as well, not that I blame them. I have turned my parents away time and time again, neglected them when my life was going well and fallen on their doorstep when I've hit tough times. I can't do that again. As for my friends? Well, I ditched my old ones in favour of the new, who didn't turn out to be friends at all. By now, everyone will know the intimate thoughts I have shared with you – this diary is my legacy to the world. I want my parents to know I love them, I want Troy to know I always did and I want Danny to know I forgive him – I am leaving this earth and I want everything to be settled before I go. Goodnight.

September 28 & 29

2.30p.m.   Botany Bay Hospital

I'm not sure if I've been to heaven or hell – but I'm back. I didn't think I'd ever write in this diary again. I wouldn't have, if it were not for Troy – he saved my life. I've just heard the full story. He found me in my apartment, unconscious. He rushed me to the hospital where they pumped my stomach. Apparently, I was clinically dead for more than a few seconds. I took so many sleeping pills this doesn't surprise me. I feel lucky to be alive. I am lucky to have a true friend like Troy who, after all this time, took the effort to seek me out – just as I was about to make my final exit. If we hadn't seen each other at the beach the other day, if he hadn't been worried enough about me to pay a visit – well, I wouldn't be here today. Mum and Dad have been at my bedside, hoping and praying I would make a full recovery. They have left me to rest. That's what I am going to do.

September 30

6.30p.m.   Mosman Manor

I am back at my parents – for good. Troy convinced me this is the best thing to do. It doesn't mean I have failed, or that I can't stand on my own two feet. It simply means I need the love and support of my family – and they need me. Troy and I talked about our relationship for the first time today. I asked him if he and Nadine were still together. I was prepared for him to answer either way. He told me they weren't. They tried to make a go of it, but in the end they realised their love was just a strong form of friendship. He has never felt for anyone the way he feels for me. He didn't suggest we get back together or pressure me in any other way. He just gave me food for thought. I'm thinking . . .

October 1

7.00p.m.   Mosman Jetty

Home is where the heart is. Mum and I spent the entire day together. We laughed and chatted like we never have before – we were friends. This near-death experience has completely changed the way I feel about my life and other people. I have made a self-discovery – life is about what you feel on the inside, not what other people perceive from the outside. And the only way to feel good on the inside is to treat people well, treat yourself well. In return, you will have all that you ever wanted, which is probably not what you thought it was in the first place. I have learned a hard lesson and I'm not going to forget it.

October 2

I know I have a friend for life – Troy. I thought long and hard about my feelings for him, whether we had a future as a couple. So much has happened between us. But it isn't love. Love is what I felt for Danny, trust is what I feel for Troy. I am grateful for everything he has done and I'm glad he is back in my life. I hope it will always be this way. As for Danny, I've got him worked out. He uses everyone to get what he wants. He saw my popularity on TV as a meal ticket to whatever he wanted, and I was naïve enough to feed him – but now I can see through him. Goodbye, Danny.

October 3

7.30p.m.   Mosman Manor

Here I go again. I have just received the opportunity of another lifetime. A hot shot agent from London, Michael West, just phoned. He got my number from the production office of *Mercy Hospital*, which has become a huge hit in the UK. It is screened twice a day to an audience of twenty million. My character, Sasha Somers,

216

has just come on air and is causing a sensation. Michael said he represents many well known artists in the UK. and if I am interested in going over, he can guarantee me high paying work. In fact, there are many opportunities in the pantomime season this Christmas and if I want he can organise a role. However, I must act fast. Michael can get me a flight straight away, all expenses paid, but I must leave in a couple of days. I didn't know what to say. The offer is too good to refuse . . . but I will be sacrificing all the progress I have made with my family. What do I do?

October 4 & 5

Today I arrived at the airport full of hopes, dreams and determination not to make the same mistakes again. As I was saying my final goodbyes, a familiar face appeared. Danny. He begged me not to go. He said he was clean. He wants to make a fresh start. I loved Danny, but I've learnt my lesson now; I shall never see him again.

We're taking off up into the sky. Whether I crash again, only time will tell.